# RIVER ROAD

## CHRIS PARISH

River Road

Copyright © 2021 Chris Parish.

Published by German Pit Publishing, LLC

ISBN (paperback): 978-1-7367877-1-7
ISBN (ebook) : 978-1-7367877-0-0

For information contact:
www.crparish.com

*For the future…*

# CONTENTS

# CHAPTER 1

# THE MYSTERIOUS NEWSPAPER

I've never met a pen that hated the color of the paper it wrote on. The paper never cared for the color of the pen's ink, either. I could say a city isn't its people, however, it is the people that make up the city. In a predominately white city, a black person stands out. The same goes for a white person in a black city. I had moved from, Harken, Texas, a black city, and moved to, Grayson, Texas, a white city, is exactly that - polar opposites. I'm not going to talk about where I came from, at least not in solitary. My mother moved us to Grayson, Texas on June 29, 1997, the day before my fourteenth birthday. Some birthday present, huh? She said we were going to have a better future in Grayson. Well, I don't know if my future would end up being any better than the future I would have gotten in Harken. So far, though, Harken didn't try to kill me, it only beat me up, and not because of my skin color, but because of the color of my clothes. I could go on and on and compare both cities, but I'll just focus on Grayson, for now. Harken is yesterday. A yesterday I'm willing to forget. However, there are some memories I have of Grayson that I would like to forget, too. I'm going to write about it now and leave it at that. Call me crazy, but I feel the reasoning behind my unfortunate experience must be shared.

On the surface, you would think Grayson was a thousand times better place than Harken. Remember that old saying, "To never judge a book by its cover?" Well, that's Grayson, Texas. On the outside looking in, you would think it's a nice quiet place to live. Which it is, I guess, if you fit in a certain criterion. If you meet that criterion, then you may never have any problems with anyone here. My mother fit in, mostly, until it came to me.

'This is my story. I'll start from the day of my birthday, not because it was my birthday but because that's the day it all started. My first day on River Road.

***

"Since when did we start receiving the newspaper?" I asked my mother when I saw her come into the house with a newspaper folded under her right arm.

"I found it in the front yard, it must be for the people that used to live here!" she said pulling the paper from her arm to take a glance at it. I thought she was going to throw it my way, but she instead hesitated for a moment. Her eyes squinted and her head cocked back, her eyes locked in on the newspaper.

"What's the matter, mom? Are there some big words you don't know? Let me see and I'll read it to you!" I said smart-alecky, reaching for the newspaper.

"No, you're not reading this one!" she said while pulling the paper away from my prying hands. She held it behind her as she walked into her room and shut the door.

Puzzled, I said, "I'm sorry, mom, I didn't mean to upset you!" I walked up to her door and knocked lightly on it with my fingertips. I jiggled the knob, "Locked!"

"You didn't upset me, Ralphie, there are just some things in this particular newspaper I'd prefer you not to see!" she said through the door, "This paper may have been for us after all."

"Then why can't I see it?" I say to my mother who has gone silent. "Mom!"

She knew I liked to read, and she would let me read anything. I didn't understand why she was doing this. I began thinking that maybe there was something in there about our family she didn't want me to know. The family that lives here in Grayson. I thought, surely, there was something in the newspaper about them. Her side of the family she didn't want me to know. My father's side I don't know all too well, except for a few double first cousins back in Harken.

Later, when my mother was at work and after I went to the library, I searched her room for that newspaper. Some of our moving boxes were still packed up so there were plenty of places to hide it. She knew her behavior piqued my interest, so she would have hidden it someplace she knew I wouldn't look. Her behavior alone fired my curiosity. The secrecy made it worth my time. I searched her bedside drawers, her panty drawer, gross! I searched her closet, nothing. She hid it well. I was going to have to search the whole entire house if I was to find the darn newspaper, including the packed boxes still sitting in the hallway and in the living room. And if I was going to do all that before she came home from work, I had to have some help to do it.

My pores soaked of sweat as the sun beat down on me while walking over to my Uncle Ronnie's house. Uncle Ronnie, unc, is my mother's brother. He lived only a few blocks away and my cousin, Aunty Charlene's son, Jaray, was living with him at the time. Aunty Charlene drank too much, so she let Jaray stay with unc. It seemed she cared more for drinking than anything else in the world.

"Hey, Ralphie, I'm sorry I couldn't help you guys yesterday." Jaray said as I walked into his room.

I sat down on the love seat that Jaray used to play his PlayStation, "It's all good, unc and his friend did most of the unloading. We still haven't unpacked everything yet. What are you doing?"

"Chillin,' was about play some PlayStation. You want to play?"

"Nah, I came over because my mother found a newspaper in our front yard..." I began to say before Jaray sat beside me and rudely cut me off, "And... people get newspapers delivered all the time!" he says while half rolling his eyes. I wanted to knock him a good one, but I knew he'd knock me a good one back. We would always be out in my front yard duking it out when he came to visit in Harken. It was fun. We'd fight until one of us started bleeding or gave up. It was usually me who started to bleed first. My mother would be so furious every time, too. He's at least a foot taller than me and a couple of years older and had maybe ten pounds on me as well. I wasn't in the mood to fight today, though. I just wanted his help finding the newspaper.

"I wanted to read it, but she wouldn't let me. She just took it off to her room and shut the door, told me I couldn't. She's never done that before. She has always let me read anything I wanted and encourages me to read, and write, all the time."

Her keeping the newspaper from me piqued Jaray's curiosity, too. "Well then," he says, "Let's find that paper!" he begins leading the way out the door to his room, through the living room and back down to my house.

"That's strange," he says, "Oh, and happy birthday, by the way."

I had forgotten about my birthday with all the searching for the mysterious newspaper.

"Thanks," I said, still concerned only for the newspaper, "Yes, it is strange, she has never acted like this before. I looked everywhere in her room and couldn't find it," I continued, trying to keep up with Jaray, taking twice as many steps as his because of his long legs.

As we were coming up to my house, I'd noticed my mother's car in the driveway.

"Aw man, my mom's home!" I say, turning to Jaray, "It's lunchtime, ain't it?"

Jaray looks at his watch, "It's 12:46."

"Good, she should be going back to work soon. She gets a lunch from twelve to one. We'll have to wait for her to leave before we can start searching, or she'll know what's up. We can play some Super Mario on my Nintendo 64 in the meantime."

"Hey Ralphie," my mother said as I walked in the front door. "Where have you been?" She put her cigarette in the ashtray, then she stood up from the kitchen chair and her tone of voice changed slightly as Jaray walked in behind me, "Jaray, good to see you, what have you been up to?" she asked, using her sweet aunt voice.

"You're so full of questions, Aunty Barb. I'm good, how are you?" Jaray answers.

"Come over here and give your aunt a hug!" she said, continuing to stand while Jaray walked over to her and gave her a hug. After he embraced her, his head rested perfectly on top of hers, her head buried in his chest, "You've gotten so tall since the last time I saw you, boy!"

"Yeah, people grow, aunty, you should try it sometime," he said gaining a pop upside the head, "You shush it!"

"So, what are you boys up to?" my mother says releasing Jaray.

A little too abruptly, I replied, "Nintendo!"

"Nintendo?" she looked at her watch, "Oh, well, I have to get back to work, I'll see you boys later, stay out of trouble, will ya!" my mother says reaching for her purse from the back of the kitchen chair.

"What kind of trouble can we get into while playing Nintendo?" I ask turning toward my bedroom.

"Ralphie, give me a hug before I go," she insisted. I walked over and hugged her, our heads side by side, "I'll make you a birthday cake when I get home, okay?"

"Okay, mom," I said, releasing her and opening the refrigerator door, and grabbed two cans of coke. Jaray had already gone into my room. I heard the front door close. I head to my bedroom and start to open the door. It swung open; the knob jerked from my hand.

"Okay, Ralphie, let's find that paper!" Jaray says, heading toward my mother's room.

"I got us a coke!" I handed him one.

"It's warm!" he hands it back.

"I think my mom just put them in the fridge. We didn't have any earlier today."

I sat both cokes down on the console table. He began to search my mother's room.

"I've already searched in here," I said to Jaray, standing in the doorway.

"Yeah, well, I haven't! You may have overlooked it. Two eyes are better than one. So, I'm going to give it a go!" he says.

I waved him off and started to search the boxes in the hall and the hall closet. I found nothing in the closet, but I had lots of boxes to search. Jaray at a slow pace comes out of my mother's room. I'm still digging through one of our moving boxes and I see him out of my peripheral. He's reading something.

"Did you know your dad is in prison?" he asks, looking down at me.

"Yeah, my mom told me. He's always been in and out of prison," I said. "It doesn't matter where he is, he never had anything to do with me, never has and probably never will," I said while putting pictures and candles back into the box I was searching through.

Standing to my feet I asked, "Did you give up searching for the newspaper?"

"No, I just found this in the mess on your mother's side table," Jaray says, trying to hand me the paper.

I shake my head, "I've already seen it, I just want the newspaper," I replied, not grabbing the paper from him. An obvious pain of not knowing a father showed. "Put it back!" I demanded.

"All right, crybaby!"

"I told you I've already searched my mom's room!"

"Shut up, you want my help or not?" Jaray asks, turning to put the paper back on my mother's side table.

"What if I said no?"

"Doesn't matter if you didn't want my help or not, I want to know what's in the newspaper, too!"

We searched everywhere in the house. Under the mattresses. Through the drawers in the bedrooms and kitchen, kitchen pantry, bathroom, boxes in the living room, even the laundry room. We took a snack break, and I searched the papers on the dining room table. Nothing. We just sat at the kitchen table soiling it with our crumbs.

The newspaper had vanished!

"Forget it Jaray, she must have thrown it away or something," I said, a little saddened. "I really wanted to know what she didn't want me to see."

"Yeah, me too. Let's go to my house, Ralphie, I'm done searching. Just ask her when she comes home."

Jaray stands, crumbs fall to the floor.

"I don't want to go anywhere; I'll see you later." I stand, following Jaray to the front door. As he opens it and walks out, I felt the warm July air breeze touch my face. The door latches shut. I stand there lost in thought. Thinking about a father I never knew, the paper I'll never see, the hot July weather. Nintendo.

"I'll just go play Super Mario," I whisper to myself.

***

A few hours later Jaray comes crashing through my front door. Luckily, nothing breaks. "Ralphie!" he yells.

"I'm on the toilet, be out in a min…" the bathroom door bursts open. Jaray pinches his nose with his right thumb and index finger and shows me a newspaper with his left hand.

"Dang, Ralphie, what did you eat!"

"You've found the paper?"

"Hurry up and finish, you've gotta see this!" he says while shutting the door leaving me to finish my business.

*** 

Entering the dining room, I could see the front and the back of the newspaper. Jaray sitting at the kitchen table, newspaper concealing his face, albeit spread open. The colors black and white, on the cover, a red rectangle enclosing a hooded person sitting on a horse holding a torch tipped with a red fiery flame. The closer I came to the paper the more things stood out. On the other side, in the rectangle, a white cross outlined in black centered in a red circle. In the center of the cross appeared to have a red blood drop. Between the hooded horseman and the white cross were the words, The Klansman.

"So, where did you find the paper?" I say pulling a chair out to sit.

Looking over the newspaper, Jaray says, "Unc had it, said your mom brought it to him this morning! There are crazy things in here, too. It's about the KKK!"

"The KKK? I've heard of the KKK, aren't they only in Mississippi, though?"

"Shoot son, haven't you read the history about Grayson? Crain's Ferry? The KKK are all over the United States, different subgroups of the Klan. Bunch of rednecks if you ask me."

"Subgroups? Sounds like the gangs back in Harken. The Bloods and Crips. They have subgroups, too."

"Nothing like that, look at what it says," Jaray says, easing the newspaper over to me.

Looking through the newspaper, it shows many signs of an invisible empire. Members hiding behind white sheets with hoods, looking like a ghost. Some others in red, black, and purple sheets. Well probably not sheets, but that's what comes to mind when I see them. It looks like they just jumped out of their bed and covered themselves with sheets with pillowcases on their heads, cutting two holes for their eyes so they could see out. Pictures of crosses burning, wording racial slurs here and there, and talking about how colors should not mix. Which also puzzled me because of the different color sheets they wore. The paper obviously does not discriminate the colors that are on it.

"See, as the gangs back in Harken, they too, have a problem with color mixing," I say, looking over a Jaray.

Jaray reaches over and nudges me while pulling the newspaper back toward him, "Ralphie, you don't know what you're talking about!"

Turning the newspaper to where he can read, "They are talking about people, different races mixing and having children, you know like us!"

"I understand that, but the gangs back in Harken don't like the colors mixing either, no matter the race. A Blood can't be over in a Crip's territory and vice versa. Even the Blood and Crip subgroups can't be around other Blood and Crip subgroups. They allow colors to divide them, just like what they are talking about in the paper."

Shaking his head, Jaray breathes in deeply, lifts the newspaper up off the table as to show me for the first time, "Someone put this in your yard because of the color of your skin, son." He sets the newspaper back on the table and points at himself, "You see, I can pass for white because my skin is practically white." Then he points to me and continues talking, "You, you can't pass for white even though your mom is white. You understand? Look, my mom is half white," he points back to himself, "Because our grandpa is white, and he said that my mom's mom, my blood grandma, is black, only light-skinned. My dad was some racist white prick who raped my mom for the fun of it, and she ended up pregnant with me." He pauses, as to catch his breath, "Abortion is a sin, so mom kept me. Your dad is a dark-skinned black man. As Tupac says, the darker the flesh the deeper the roots. Look at you, you're not dark-skinned, but you're not as light as me."

"I know," I said shaking my head because he always likes to reference rap song lyrics.

"These people put this paper in your yard to try and scare you guys, they are trying to prove something."

I look down at the cover of the newspaper and read something about them fighting not for glory nor riches, I look up at Jaray, then back down at the newspaper and read some more, but for freedom. "What are they trying to prove?"

Jaray stands, and slowly pushes the kitchen chair back under the table, because my mother preaches about doing that all the time when we lived in Harken, "I don't know," Jaray says, "I'll figure something out. They are not going to try and intimidate my family."

The squeak of the front door opening caught our attention, our heads turned toward the living room. My mother struggling to carry grocery bags as she walks through the door. "Hey, what are you boys doing, are you going to even get up and help?" Her eyes went from me to Jaray, our chair screamed as we rose to help. As my mother walked into the kitchen her eyes scanned what we were looking at on the table,

"Ralphie," she began saying, laying the bags on the counter, "I didn't want you to see that! Jaray, why did you bring that back over here?" Tears hung in her eyes, her voice cracking as she spoke.

"Sorry, Aunty Barb, Ralphie just wouldn't stop talking about it. And I wanted to know what was in it, too!"

"Mom, it's okay, I know a little bit about that stuff."

"It's not okay, and I'm sure you do, but that stuff has always been distant from us." She says walking closer to us, reaching for the newspaper, grabs it up and to read something from the cover, "This is ridiculous!"

"I don't think it has been distant from us, mom, the gangs back in Harken are like that, too. They have problems with different colors. Remember when the Crips jumped me for wearing red in their neighborhood on my way to school? What's the difference? I'm not a gang member and yet they still beat me up."

"I see where you're going with the color thing!" Jaray says, "In a way, they are the same."

"No difference, I was jumped because of the color of my clothes, there, and now I'm targeted because of the color of my skin, here. No difference to me, all the same. White people, black people, still people."

My mother lays the paper back on the table and draws me close for a hug, "I'm sorry, Ralphie, I shouldn't try to shield you from all this, you're so smart with all that reading. I should have known you would already be familiar with racism."

I pulled myself free from her hug, "What are we going to do about this, mom?"

"Nothing, we'll do absolutely nothing, that goes for you too, Jaray, nothing. We will not let them intimidate us."

"Aunty Barb, we have to do something, we can't just let this go on!"

"We're not going to let it go on, but not another word, give me that paper!" Mother takes the paper, "No more reading this crap, go play Nintendo or something while I make your birthday cake."

"Who can play Nintendo right now, mom? There is no way I'll be able to concentrate."

"Nothing more, Ralphie, I mean it!"

"Come on, Ralph, let's go for a walk. Let your mom cool off, she can keep the paper!"

I looked at Jaray and then at my mom, "Maybe my mom's right, we should just drop it. We don't want them to have any power over us, over our thinking. If we go after them, they'll come back after us. You know revenge is a revolving door," I said, pausing only for a second when Jaray said, "Revenge is best served cold!" His eyes wide and his mind obviously focused on something else. "As for the walk," I continued, "Let's do that, I could use a walk, maybe we can stop by the library again!"

# CHAPTER 2

# THE PREACHERS SERMON

The newspaper, bouncing around in my head from a couple of days ago. Bouncing like the basketball bouncing I hear, somewhere close. Bounce, silence, bounce, bounce. I came around the corner of the Free Assembly Church of God, and there I'd found the culprit. A white kid shooting a basketball into a basketball goal. A white kid I would soon find a friend in. A friendship that could last the rest of my life.

"Hey, could I shoot some hoops with you?" I asked, easing my way closer to the white kid.

"Sure, let's play horse. I must warn you, though, I play all the time," he says passing me the ball. I catch it and push in on the ball with both hands, as to check the air pressure.

"I'm Ralph, but everyone calls me, Ralphie."

"Hey, Ralphie, my name's Daron, everyone calls me Daron."

"Daron, do you go to church here?"

"Yeah, my dad is the pastor here. He is getting ready for tonight's service," he says, both hands extended in front of him pointing toward the big church.

Daron was a fragile kid. He could bend his fingers back and have them touch the top of his forearm. Probably helped him with playing basketball. It would sicken me when he'd do it, so he did it a lot, just to irritate me.

I've never been able to play basketball well in my life and that didn't bother me today as we started playing horse. I just wanted something to do and a friend to do that something with. Today, basketball was that something. Daron was that friend.

I shot the ball toward the hoop and made it, could have been a three-pointer. Daron, swallowing hard. I could see his Adam's apple rise and settle back down. He had caught the rebound and made his way to where I was standing. He pulled the same shot, swoop! Much more technique in his shot than I had in mine. Nothing but net. No letter, none. Smiling I've realized that this game of horse may take a while. I have nothing better to do anyway. Daron took it upon himself to go and grab his own rebound.

"Where are you from?" Daron asked, passing me the ball, "I haven't seen you around here before!"

"I'm from Harken, just moved here on Sunday. My mom is supposed to be checking me into school in the next couple of weeks during school enrollment. She says they start back in August." Daron shook his head in agreement. I settled my breath, tried another three-point shot, and missed, the ball bounced off the backboard right into Daron's hands. A smile crossed his freckled face.

"Get ready H man!" he says while shooting from the same distance I was shooting from. Swoop! Nothing but net.

"Man, you're good!" I told him while I got the rebound.

"I told you I play all the time!"

I make my way to him, bouncing the ball a few times. I turn and try and mimic the shot he had made and scored nothing but H.

"All right, Ralphie, time to make a HO out of you!" he said while setting up his shot. Closer to the goal this time, he steadies his breath, lines up his shot, then shoots. Swoop! Nothing but net! I think he may have been taking it easy on me. It didn't matter, though, I'd missed the shot anyway. He didn't let me hear the end of it either. I've never been called a HO before in my life. The way he was saying it, you'd think HO was my name, at least until I became a HOR.

"Daron, we have to get going now!" his father said coming around the corner, "Who's your friend?" he continues after spotting me.

"That's Ralphie, he just moved here!" Daron answers.

"Nice to meet you, Ralphie, I'm Pastor Mike!"

I extended my right hand and shake Pastor Mike's hand, "It's nice to meet you, too, Pastor."

Pastor Mike released my hand and said, "Come to church with us tonight or on Sunday," and before I could give an answer he continued, "I'll even come and pick you up, how's that sound?"

"Sure, not tonight, though, on Sunday, sure, I live on River Road in the…" I began to say before he interrupted.

"I know where you live, I'll pick you up Sunday then. Let me pray for you kids really quick before we go, does that sound okay?"

I'd noticed he only looked at me for an answer, "Sure!" I said, puzzled, thinking about how he knew where I lived and still asked his son who I was anyway. Standing in my confusion, he began to pray, I closed my eyes and bowed my head.

"Father, thank you for bringing us together and using the sport of basketball to do so. I ask that you continue to bring people together using any device you deem worthy. Lord, I ask in your name, that you bless Ralphie's life and build a strong bond between him and Daron, I ask in closing, Lord, that you help battle the evil thrown our way. Lord, our hearts are yours to do as you will, in Jesus's name, amen."

"Amen!"

"Amen," I say while raising my head and opening my eyes.

"Do you need a ride somewhere, Ralphie?" the pastor asks.

"No, I'm just going to walk over to my cousin's house. Thanks, anyway!"

"Okay, Ralphie, we'll see you Sunday, I'll pick you up at 8 am," he says, putting his arm around Daron as they began to walk to their car.

"Okay, see you then."

While I walked over to see Jaray, I couldn't figure out how the pastor knew where I live. My mother didn't go to church, in fact, none of my family did. Not anymore anyway since my grandmother had passed. She'd be proud that I was going, at least this coming Sunday, anyway. There's no way he knew where I lived and if he knew then surely Daron knew as well. I came up to the door of unc's house, I went to knock on the door, but it opened.

"Aah!"

"Sorry, Aunty Janie. I didn't mean to startle you. Is Jaray here?"

"Oh Ralphie, yes, he's in his room. I've got to get to work, go on in!"

I walk in and head to Jaray's room and knock on the door. Tupac's My Ambitionz Az a Ridah was playing loudly. I wasn't sure if he had heard me knocking, I knocked again.

"Go away!" he says.

"Jaray, it's me, Ralphie!"

"Oh, hold up!"

I could hear him rapping in line with Tupac the closer he got to the door, something about opening fire, seeing people kill him, as they witnessed his steel. Spitting at adversaries, and them being envious and coming after him. Tupac was a great rapper.

"Whatcha doing, Ralphie?" he asks, after he swung the door open. He then walks toward the stereo and turns it down about halfway.

"I was just playing basketball with Daron at the Free Assembly, and his dad the pastor wants me to go to church with them on Sunday. He said he'd give me a ride. I was about to tell them where I live, and he said he already knew. The thing is, I just met them," I said, still wondering how the pastor knew where I lived.

"Son, you gotta understand something, you are the only noticeable colored kid in town. You stand out here. People notice and people talk, especially those who have a problem with color." Jaray, his grimaced face letting me know what he has just said was reality.

"Are you saying that they are racist?"

"No, I'm saying, Daron's dad, being a pastor hears different people talk all the time. He's their pastor. Some people think that we shouldn't be mixed around with white folks. That's just how most people around here were raised. But forget all that, don't let people control your thoughts."

"Yeah, you're right! What are ya up to?"

"Chillin' got some Pac on and everyone's gone so, I figured I'd blast the stereo."

"Aunty Janie just left," I said, pointing with my thumb toward the front of the house.

"Yeah, I know, that's why I just turned it up! Right before you started beating down my door like a maniac!" Jaray said, laughing.

Jaray and I hung out the rest of the evening, listening to music. Jaray is really into music. He talked about being a rapper. He would often joke about being the first big-time *white* rapper. That could never happen of course, and I don't think he would be able to compete with Eminem, a white rapper who ended up being signed by Dr. Dre.

"I'm going to head home, mom's probably making supper. You want to come?"

"Nah, Aunty Janie told me to go up to the store and she'll get me something," Jaray said as he started changing the CD, then he stopped and looked back at me, "Ralphie, forget about that racism stuff, it'll only eat you up inside and like grandma used to say, 'It makes way for the devil!'"

Shaking my head, I recalled a time she had said that to me, and I left Jaray and headed home. Jaray was probably right, though, but I couldn't help it. Racism really bothered me. What does the color of someone's skin have to do with anything? What does the color of someone's clothes have to do with anything? Pondering those questions really began eating at me.

I was almost home when I could see my mother through the kitchen window. She must be making supper, I thought. As I got closer, my sense of smell told me she was. I could use a nice hot meal right about now. I opened the front door and my mother said, "I just called Jaray to see if you were there and here you are."

"What are we eating?" I spoke.

"Fried pork chops, green beans, mashed potatoes, gravy, and cornbread. Have a seat, it's about ready," she said, grabbing a plate from the counter and dropping everything from the four-course meal on it. "Do you want some iced tea?"

"Do I? Yes, please!" I said, then realized, I haven't even thought about anything to drink since before playing basketball. Talking between bites of my pork shop I said, "I met a kid today, his name is Daron. His dad is the pastor of the Free Assembly of God church, Pastor Mike. We played basketball, Daron and me. His dad invited me to church on Sunday, and even said he'd pick me up. I went to tell him where we live but he said he'd already known. Which was weird since I had just met them. Jaray says it's because I am basically the only colored kid here and everyone talks, especially to a pastor!"

"Jaray is probably right. I hate that people are like that. Judging people's skin color," she said, her voice saddened.

"It's not just skin color, mom, you know that. We had to deal with those gangs in Harken because I wore the wrong color in their neighborhood. They jumped me and warned me not to come back with those colors. It's just stupid." I continued to eat; my mother's head shook in agreement. We finished the rest of our dinner in silence. I think we both needed it.

Before going to bed my mother spoke softly to me, "Ralph, I'm sorry you're experiencing racism. But remember, people have had it worse and those who care for you are not judging you at all, and you shouldn't worry about what others think."

"Good night, mom!"

I anxiously waited for Sunday morning to come, but not to go to church, though. Daron, the only friend I had in town, that wasn't family, went to that church and I didn't know where he lived. No going anywhere for the next couple of days, Jaray and unc came over with some fireworks. Independence Day. Aunty Janie worked so much she couldn't be there. Mom didn't come outside but once, and she didn't seem interested in any of the fireworks. Unc, Jaray and I spent Friday night popping fireworks on the road, until we ran out. But the nice part about it, though, is that I lived toward the end of River Road, and so many people came all the way down to pop their fireworks. We would listen to their music and watch their fireworks, such a nice free show and a fun way to celebrate our freedom. Jaray spent the night and we didn't go to sleep until three in the morning. My mother had to come into my room and tell us to go to bed. Her mouth never fully opened when she told us either, she spoke directly from her teeth.

When I woke up on Saturday, Jaray had already left. Mom said he had things to do. That's just something he would say when he wanted to go. I don't blame him for leaving either, he has that nice big stereo in his room and all those CDs. I'd spent most of the day reading my library book, *Killing Floor.* I wanted to return it on Monday, so I had to finish it quickly.

When Sunday came, I was ready, dressed in the best clothes I had. Khaki slacks, a little too big around the waist, a blue button-up Ralph Lauren polo sport shirt with an American flag covering the heart. My mother, smiling, her heart happy that I was going to church. And me, happy that I had a friend. She took out her polaroid and snapped a picture.

"Mom, it's not a date, it's just church," I said, moving the camera away with my left hand and snatching the picture with my right. I fanned it a few times and looked at it. I thought I looked sharp.

"I look sharp!"

"Yes, you do!" she said, "Now give me the picture!"

I heard a few honks, and I handed the picture to my mother, and looked out the window. I saw Pastor Mike and Daron making their way to the front door. I swung the door open just before he made it on the porch.

"Hey, Ralphie, you ready?" Daron asked as I walked out the door.

"Yeah!"

On our drive to church, I had told Daron and Pastor Mike about my weekend and that I almost finished reading *Killer Floor*. Pastor Mike said he reads but only of the Christian genre. I thought it may be putting himself in a box. You can learn so much more by reading widely.

At church, while Pastor Mike was greeting churchgoers as they came in, Daron gave me a tour. From the sound of things, Daron wanted to be like his father and become a pastor.

"Hey Jarod, meet Ralphie, he just moved here!" Daron said to another white kid. Taller than the both of us, bushy blond hair, styled like Einstein's.

"Nice to meet you Ralphie, I'm Jarod!" he said waving at me. My first thought was he didn't want to shake my hand because I wasn't white. Then when his hand came down from the wave, he extended it to shake. I shook.

"Nice to meet you, too!"

We made our way to our pew. The three of us set together in the front pew. Pastor Mike made his way to center stage, the pulpit as they call it, to begin his morning sermon.

"God is good!"

I could hear the people in the pews behind us reply in unison,

"Amen."

"All the time."

"Yes, he is!" Then silence entered the church as if the Holy Spirit began walking down the aisle and to enter Pastor Mike, who began preaching and didn't stop for quite a while.

"Most of you know I was born here in Grayson. I'm not going to say how long ago to not give away my incredibly young age of twenty-seven!"

Many laughs came from the pews because it was obvious Pastor Mike was not twenty-seven.

"My mother and father were not in my profession," he continued, "But they alone taught me to go to God for guidance as some of you know all too well. They would minister to some of you here in this very room, many years ago. I love and miss them; may they rest with God in peace," the pastor preached looking around the church from the pulpit. Members speaking up in agreement.

"Amen, praise God!"

"In Matthew five thirteen, Jesus says that we are the salt of the earth." Pastor Mike, went on to preach, "But if the salt loses its saltiness, how can it be made salty again? Living here in Grayson we know this well. If salt loses its saltiness it is to be thrown out and trampled underfoot. Don't lose your flavor and be trampled on. Don't become under the power of the evil one. Be the salt of the earth as Jesus wants us to be."

Many people believe that the preacher is preaching to them because they relate the preaching to their situation. I too, felt the same way. God must have been speaking to me through Pastor Mike. He preached some more but I was lost in thought about salt and how it lost its flavor. Somehow, I'd felt that I was losing my saltiness and I didn't know how to keep it from happening. Still lost in thought, I had noticed a couple of men on the same pew as us rise and then they headed toward the front doors. No one seemed to pay them any mind, except for me. Probably because Pastor Mike was in prayer, and here I am looking around and wondering what these guys were up to. I thought that maybe they were leaving. When those two made it to the front doors, they just opened the doors and stood there.

"Amen," Pastor Mike said, ending his prayer. Everyone began to rise, and Pastor Mike thanked them while walking himself toward the front doors. He paused his footsteps a few times, shaking and hugging with those in the congregation. When he made it to the front doors, he stopped there, thanked everyone for coming as they walked out to enjoy the rest of their day. He asked them to return that evening for another sermon. He even thanked me, Daron, and Jarod as we walked out. I don't think I'll be coming tonight, I thought to myself. I still need to process what I had heard this morning.

"We are going for a walk!" Daron told his father. Pastor Mike nodded his head to say it was okay.

I couldn't shake the salt thoughts and spoke up, "What do you guys think about salt losing its saltiness?"

"Sprinkle some salt on the fries and they'll taste better, but if the salt loses its saltiness, it would ruin the fries," Jarod said, giggling.

"Yeah, you would have to throw them out," Daron included.

"So, what does that mean for us, you know, people?" I questioned.

Jarod then answered, "Jesus says that people, especially Christians, are the salt of the earth. We spread our saltiness on others, which means, our good manners and good characteristics. If you lose your saltiness…"

"You're basically no good, or up to no good?" I suggested, trying to finish his sentence.

"Yes, pretty much. You become a flavorless salt," Jarod said.

"I didn't even know salt could lose its flavor," I said, shrugging my shoulders.

"I have an idea," Daron says, "Let's go to the Salt Palace and see what we can find out about salt over there."

"Okay!" Jarod agrees and goes on to say, "I can't be out too long though, my granny is making lunch, do you guys wanna come? I'm sure she'll be okay with it; she loves feeding people!"

"I could use some food!" I said, looking at Daron.

"You know I'm down; I love granny's cooking!"

"What's the Salt Palace?" I asked, thinking about the food Jarod's granny would make.

Daron turned to me, "It's a museum about the salt mine here in town. The mine is under our feet. The Salt Palace is basically made up of salt, you could lick the side of it if you want. A lot of people do."

"I think I will pass."

# CHAPTER 3

# A SALTY SITUATION

The Salt Palace wasn't a very big place. The building was about fifty-by-fifty, a building with a restroom the size of a port-a-potty. The outside, faded from the weather, the salt rocks like crystals. I fought off the urge to go and lick one of them. The closer we got, the bigger the urge I had to go lick one. Daron opened the front door and held it open for Jarod and me. We entered; behind the counter I could see an elderly looking man. He looked up and closed his eyes, then shook his head, as if he were saying no for some odd reason. Daron followed us in, we all split up looking at different areas. I began reading about how the Native Americans used the local salt over one hundred years ago and how Roman soldiers were paid in salt and how the word salary came from the word salt because of how the soldiers were paid with it. The man behind the counter spoke up, "Anything I can help you with?"

"No sir!" Daron said, still looking and reading the history on the salt mine, not even taking the courtesy to look up at the elderly man. I looked up, and I saw the old man and he was not looking at Daron or Jarod, he was looking at me. Daron then said, "We're just looking around!" The man obviously not satisfied with Daron's answer questions us again.

"Don't you have anything better to do than to bug an old man?" Or more likely, he questioned me.

"I just moved here and don't know of anything else to do!" I said, a little too hesitantly.

"Maybe you shouldn't have moved here, then, boy!" the man said, his face grimaced. An angry look in his face and his eyes piercing mine, "We don't need the likes of you here anyway!" My blood began to boil. I knew he was talking about my skin color. What is it with this city and the color of someone's skin? It seems I can't shake the racism here no matter how hard I try. My anger hitting me like rain on the concrete, I thought of my granny Moore, she told me once that anger is the foothold of the devil. I looked over at Daron, "Let's get out of here!" I turned and walked out, pushing the glass door so hard, I feared it would break. Luckily, it didn't. Maybe I should have broken it, I probably would have felt much better.

Daron and Jarod didn't follow me out, immediately. I first thought they probably weren't offended as I was. They did come out a few minutes later, though. "Don't worry about that lazy piece of cow's dung," Daron said, looking and pointing toward the Salt Palace, "He just thinks he owns this city!"

"What did he say when I left?" I asked, blood still boiling.

"He called us a few names I'm not repeating. We called him a few names; I'm also not going to repeat!" Jarod said.

Daron spotted the man's car, "Come on that's his car right there," jogging over to it. He stopped right in front of it. Leaned his torso and head back, hocked a loogie and spit it right on the middle of the windshield. The bell on the Salt Palace door rang, "Hey!" the old man yelled. We all started to run. I could hear him scream, "Niggers!" We got a block down the road and slowed to a walk.

"I hate people like that!" Daron said, "My dad says they work for the devil and don't even realize it."

"Did he say what I think he said?" I asked, catching my breath, "He called us niggers!"

"Yeah, he called us something similar after you walked out," Jarod said, also catching his breath, "Let's get to my granny's and get some of that good food she's probably already cooking."

"Amen to that!" Daron agreed, looking up at the sky as if he were talking to God.

"You know it has been like that since I've moved here. Someone threw a Klan newspaper in my yard the other day."

Daron stopped, "What the...really?" he said, shaking his head, "We should tell my dad what's going on, maybe he can help."

"Maybe he can, maybe he can't, it's not going to stop them from being racist!" Jarod said, "Let's just get to my granny's, she'll know what to do."

As we arrived at Jarod's granny's house, we could already smell the food. Mixed flavors reaching our nostrils, watering our mouths. Jarod opened the front door, and we heard his granny say, "Jarod, is that you coming in my door? You better have brought an empty stomach!"

"Brought three of 'em, granny!"

"Good, cause this stew is too delicious to go to the dogs," she said, pointing to the two tiny dogs sitting beside her, watching her every move hoping she would drop something. "I know Daron, that knucklehead, who's your other friend?"

"That's Ralphie, met him at church this morning."

"Where you should have been, granny!" Daron added.

"Shut it, I haven't been to church since I was a kid and I don't plan on going now, God knows where I stand and where my heart is. I don't need to go to church to prove anything.

Now grab some bowls and sit down there. Nice to meet you Ralphie, you can call me granny, and you better eat all you can, you hear me?"

"Yes ma'am, nice to meet you, too!" I waved and sat down. My mouth watering even more now that I've seen the food. Anxious to get to eat because I hadn't had breakfast.

"Grab some glasses too, Daron, and pour us some tea! Ice is in the freezer," granny says, as she pulled the stew from the stove bringing it to the kitchen table. "Careful boys, she's hot!" I could see the steam still chasing itself, reaching for the ceiling, before evaporating.

Jarod, grabbing the bowls from Daron, sat my bowl in front of me, then Daron's next to mine. Granny was already dropping stew in the bowls, Jarod grabbed the tongs, picked up the bread from the bar and brought everyone a plate with two pieces of bread. "My granny makes the best bread in the world! No lie! Isn't that right, Granny?" Jarod says, smiling, picking up his bread and dipping it into his stew.

"Boy, you know you better say grace before you bite into the bread!" granny said, pointing the ladle, still dripping with stew, at Jarod.

"Sorry, granny," he started, we all closed our eyes and bowed our heads, "Lord, thank you for bringing us to the table to feed not only our stomachs but our souls. Help us with this battle the evil one has brought upon Ralphie here lately. We have his back and, for what brought us together, Lord, bless this food granny has prepared for us, thank you, amen!"

"Amen," I said, before Daron said, "Pig out!" I thought Granny was going to back hand him, but she paused and called him a knucklehead. Daron flinched, and smirked at her.

"What's this about a battle, Ralphie?" she said, grabbing her spoon and bread as she started eating her stew.

"Well, ma'am, granny, it seems that ever since I've moved here, racism has been at my door, literally. Here, it seems I cannot please their color code!"

"Son, some people don't understand the world as it is. They only like the world they were born into. Here, the world they are born into is white and they fear that their little world will disappear. And it will, but sadly, that will be when Jesus comes," granny said, reaching for the ladle to spoon some more stew in her bowl, "I hope you don't let them eat at your core, because they will."

"My cousin said something similar the other day. Warning not to let it eat away at me."

"Yeppers, he's right. Let's eat and then we'll talk about what we can do, prepare for battle, if you will!"

"Okay, granny."

"What else have you boys been up to, since church? You act like you're starving!" Granny says, with her mouth full of bread, only pushed to one side. Her spoon was full of her next bite of stew, which she quickly devoured after questioning us.

"We went to the Salt Palace. Dad was preaching about salt and we decided to read up on the salt around here. Only we didn't get to read too long before the old man started in on us!" Daron said, then started drinking from his bowl as if it were a cup.

"E. W.? What did that old man start in on you for?" granny asked.

"Was wondering what we were doing and said Ralphie shouldn't have moved here, called us some names, and chased us down the street!" Jarod said, grabbing the ladle to fill his bowl a second time.

"Calling you boys names, huh?"

"Yeah, seems the ol' devil is after me using people who don't like color, I guess. Someone even threw a Klan newspaper in my yard the other day."

"The Klan! Oh boy, those stupid idiots. They have nothing better to do than to terrorize young kids. I remember…" granny began saying, then thinking about how terrible the story would be. "Well it doesn't matter. I'll take care of the old fart at the Salt Palace if you want me to! Looks like there is something that needs done!"

"Nah, granny, it's okay. We shouldn't let others control our emotions," I said, dipping my bread in my stew.

"Smart kid, no you shouldn't let it get to you," she agreed.

"Granny, you have to give mom this recipe. I think dad would love this stew!" Daron said, then started drinking from his bowl again. He finished it, grabbed his tea glass and finished it, stood and brought the bowl and glass to the sink. Jarod then asked, "Are you done, Ralphie?"

"Yeah, that was good, thanks granny!"

"You're very welcome, Ralphie, and you're welcome to come anytime. With or without these two knuckleheads. Now, let's prepare for battle!"

Granny began explaining, "Jesus teaches us to turn the other cheek, to love our neighbor, not an eye for an eye. These guys act like they love Jesus and do what he says, but when it comes to colored folk, they think none of that applies. That's where you get them, you see, you do what Jesus teaches us, and you apply it with everyone. You turn the other cheek and love them. When they keep coming at you, you defend what is yours, including your life. It's justified in the eyes of the Lord at that point."

"That's a really good strategy, granny. You really think they are going to keep coming after me?" I asked, swallowing hard.

"They don't want you here in their perfect little white town," she answered, "Now, as for E. W. I will call and have a little talk with him."

"Nah, you don't have too, but thanks, granny!" I told her.

"Yeah, granny, thanks for feeding us knuckleheads!" Daron added.

"Let's go walk around, guys!" Jarod says.

"You boys be careful!"

We left granny's and headed towards downtown, not by the Salt Palace. We had enough of that place for one day. We made our way by the convenience store Aunty Janie works at. I could see her inside behind the counter. She waved, I waved back. Then she waved me in.

"Hey guys, my aunt wants me to come into the store, I'll be right back!"

"We'll go with you," Jarod says, Daron followed behind.

"Ralphie, I was told you were causing trouble at the Salt Palace today!" Aunty Janie said when I walked in the store.

"Not true…"

"No, it's not true, he didn't do anything, we were just reading and looking around the Salt Palace, and the old man started saying Ralphie shouldn't have moved here," Daron interrupted.

"Yeah, he even called me a nigger!"

"He called all of us that and some other names!" Jarod added.

"Well, the word right now, from Officer Madison, is that you were causing trouble and tried to break the door to the Salt Palace and damaged E.W.'s car."

"I didn't do anything like that!"

"I spit on his windshield, that was it!" Daron admitted.

"Well, the officer is looking for you guys, you probably should go home, all of you, just to be on the safe side."

"This isn't right, Aunty Janie, I didn't do anything wrong!" I said, feeling more violated than angry. I began thinking about how anybody can be so hateful and lie saying we did things we didn't do. Now for the first time, I felt I would be better off in Harken, with the gangs, at least with them I could camouflage myself, and walk among them. Here, I stood out, had a target strapped to my back. If my mother could have found a job there that paid as well as this one here, we would have stayed in Harken. I wouldn't be a target for racism.

Daron's dad pulled up to the convenience store and a police car pulled in beside him. I immediately stiffened. I didn't know how to act. I didn't do anything wrong and yet I felt I was going to be arrested. I've never been in trouble with the police before. I got to thinking about my dad being in prison. What would he have done in a similar situation? What was prison like? Would I be able to see my family? I didn't even do anything. What was I worried about? My granny used to say, 'Worrying doesn't add one day to your life, it subtracts from it.' The thought calmed me. The officer and Pastor Mike walked it, the bell on the door dinged. Pastor Mike and the officer nodded to Aunty Janie, who nodded back.

"Boys, I was told you guys were harassing E.W. down at the Salt Palace after church this morning," the pastor said, while looking at all of us. He never once singled any of us out.

"Dad, it's all lies. We didn't do anything to that old man. He just started calling us names!"

"Yeah, Mike, that's true. He started telling Ralphie he shouldn't have moved here and to basically go back where he came from, then he called us names," Jarod agreed, repeating the same story we've been telling everyone. Seems like my skin color has shined a light on a world of hate here in Grayson, Texas.

"We didn't do anything, Pastor Mike," I added, looking at him. He was about to say something, but the officers spoke before he could.

"Now boys, it's been reported that you damaged his vehicle."

"We, we didn't damage anything, sir!" Daron said, "I..." pointing to himself, "I spit on his windshield, that's it, and it wipes off!"

"Daron, now son..." Pastor Mike began to say.

"I'm sorry, Dad, but you didn't see how he was treating us or hear the names he was calling us!"

"Well, you know that wasn't right, not justifiable," the pastor concluded.

"You're all going to have to come down the station and be questioned, one by one, with your parents, of course," the officer stated.

"I'll take them, Officer Madison, I'll call Jarod and Ralphie's parents to meet us there, they don't need to be seen getting in your vehicle," Pastor Mike demanded.

"Okay, Pastor, I'm going there now!"

"We will be there, right behind you, Janie, could I use your phone?" Pastor Mike asked, looking at Aunty Janie, who then handed him the cordless phone. He dialed Jarod's granny's phone number after putting the phone on speaker.

Ring!

Ring!

"Hello, this is granny!"

"Granny, this is Pastor Mike…"

"I'm not going to church, pastor, give it up!"

"No, this call is not about that, it's Jarod. It's been reported the boys damaged E.W.'s car and they'd like to question them down at the station."

"Oh, well, well, I just talked to E.W. and he didn't say such a thing. That lying sack of - he probably deserved it. I'll head to the station now!"

"Thanks, granny, I'll see you there!"

"Janie, could you get a hold of Ralphie's mother and have her meet us at the station?" Pastor Mike said, hanging the phone up and handing the cordless back to Aunty Janie.

"Yeah, I'll call her work phone."

Pastor thanked her and we all headed out of the store and were getting in the pastor's car when someone yelled, "Don't let the sun set on your black ass!"

The officer yelled, "Hey! That's enough!"

When we all were seated and buckled in, Pastor Mike drove us to the police station. Granny had already made it there. My mother worked just outside of town and would take a few minutes longer. I could see E.W. standing outside the station. Granny was getting out of her car and I could see she was talking, probably to E.W. because he was looking at her, shaking his head, just as he did when we entered the Salt Palace.

In the station we all sat around empty desks. Officer Madison asked another officer, Officer Stanley, to take Daron and Pastor Mike to an interview room. Pastor Mike, holding on to Daron's shoulder's as if to guide him, walked into the interrogation room, Officer Stanley led them in, and out of sight. Granny and Jarod were next. They, too, were escorted into an interrogation room. I sat there, looking around, waiting on my mother to show up. I wondered what all this was truly about. There was no reason to question us here. They were making a big deal out of nothing, a little spit could be wiped off, words could linger, but no one was physically harmed.

"You want something to drink? Ralph, is it?" Officer Madison asked.

"Ralphie," I corrected him, even though I was actually Ralph. "Yeah, sure, I could use a drink!"

"Okay, Ralphie, how's a root beer sound?"

"Sound's fine, thanks!"

"I'm sure your mother will be here shortly, traffic isn't that bad this time of day out there," he said. "Where did E.W. go?"

I looked around and didn't see anyone, only the officer standing there.

"I didn't see him come in," I said to Officer Madison who then went and opened the door and looked outside. He came back in and never said anything to me, he walked past me into the interrogation room where Officer Stanley was talking with Daron and Pastor Mike. I could hear them talking.

"Give us one moment, please!" Officer Madison said, motioning Officer Stanley out of the interrogation room. "E.W. isn't out there. Do you know where he went?"

"No, he mentioned smoking a cigarette and then coming right in," Officer Stanley recalled.

Ring!

Ring!

Officer Madison rushed over the phone sitting on his desk, "Grayson Police Department, Officer Madison speaking...uh-huh," he began writing something down.

"Okay, we'll be right on it." After hanging up he started speaking to Officer Stanley, "We have a car accident out on twenty-seven, at mile marker eighteen," he said. "Release everyone, we'll have to return this at a later time."

# CHAPTER 4

# A CAR WRECK

I caught a ride home with Pastor Mike and Daron. Jarod went home with his grandmother. Of course, she didn't leave without a hassle.

"You had us come up here and now you're not even going to talk to us?" she asked.

"Ma'am, we have an accident we need to report to, I'm sorry, but someone's life is on the line," Officer Madison stated.

"Well, just do your duty, then, call my lawyer next time you want to talk, let's go, Jarod!"

Pastor Mike didn't intervene. I could see him biting his tongue, though. Daron and Jarod were smirking. The officers walked us out of the front door. Still no E.W. anywhere.

*** 

When they dropped me off at home, I'd noticed my mother wasn't there, but she had been. She must have had lunch and was probably getting to work when Aunt Janie called her. She was probably hysterical when she got the call, too. She worries too much, as a mother should. Mothers are a lot like the police; always assuming the worst possible thing first.

I decided I would just play Nintendo for a while. I had already filled my stomach with granny's stew and homemade bread, so I wasn't hungry. The root beer I got from the police station wasn't very tasty and it left a nasty taste in my mouth, so I made a glass of sweetened iced tea. I noticed the dining room clock was closing in on two-thirty and I still haven't heard anything from my mother. I figured she would be popping by because I wasn't at the police station anymore. Even if they told her they would talk to us later, she still would have come home and talked to me.

While I was playing Nintendo, I thought momentarily about going to unc's house and hanging out with Jaray. The Super Mario game wasn't fulfilling my expectations at the moment. I kept zoning out and Mario would just stand there. He may have been checking his watch, waiting for me to push a button.

Knock, Knock!

Someone had knocked on the front door and pulled me out of a trance.

Knock, knock, knock!

I knew it wasn't my mother because she wouldn't have knocked.

"I'm coming!"

"Knock, knock, knock, knock, knock!"

"Ralphie!"

I opened the door. Jaray was standing there and seemed to be in a panic. My unc's car in the driveway, no one inside. Jaray must have driven himself over. Unc would let him drive periodically when he was either too busy with something else or didn't want to go anywhere. At the look of Jaray's face, I knew unc was busy with something else.

"What's going on? Are you alright?" I asked, looking at Jaray. My heart may have been trying to step in the same beat as his because my voice cracked. The emotion was taking over. Fear, maybe, of what Jaray was about to tell me.

"You have to come with me," he said, "Your mo…" a tear dropping from his left eyelid, "Your mom has been in a car wreck."

"What!" the flood gates that held tears crumbled under the words, a car wreck. "Where is she? Is she okay?"

"She's at the hospital, unc is up there now and Aunty Janie is trying to get someone to cover her so she can get up there, too." Jaray, grabbed my shirt, "Come on!"

I hadn't even realized we were still standing on the front porch. I pulled the door shut, didn't even check to make sure the door was locked. We got into the car, me in shotgun and Jaray driving, he backed out into the road. Then I heard a crash as my entire body jerked toward the driver seat.

I looked over at Jaray, "What the heck was that?" He was just as puzzled as I was. "Did you hit something?" Jaray's eyes grew three sizes as he looked past me. Everything went dark.

# CHAPTER 5

# THE LYNCHING

Ahh! A pounding headache. There's something over my head. I'm lying down. I felt like I had been hit with a baseball bat. My eyes are open, yet I can't see anything. I try to reach my head to feel around, but I can't move my hands. Duct tape? I'm duct taped, I thought to myself.

I could feel something pulling around my neck, is someone about to choke me? My mind still trying to figure out what's going on.

"Jaray, where's Jaray? Hello?"

No answer.

The pulling around my neck grew tighter. I struggled. The pulling around my neck, tightening even more. My whole body begins to move, pulled by my neck, pulled by what was possibly a rope. I begin to rise, the pulling brings my torso up, then butt, then my legs are suspended in the air. Someone was hanging me. A modern-day lynching. I struggled some more, trying to free my hands to grab at my neck, the pressure so great. Death knocking at my door. I struggle some more. The rope tightens even more. I could hear tree limbs cracking, water flowing across rocks. More pain, in my throat, this time. My eyes feel like they want to jump out of their sockets. More limbs cracking. Water flowing. Cracking.

"I can't hold on any longer!" a voice says.

"Tie it to a tree limb!" another voice shouts back.

Cracking. Water flow. Pain. I'm falling. Water! I'm underwater, my mind noticing the water surrounding my being. Maybe this is death? The tape around my hands begin to loosen up, enough to where I can free my hands. I pull them apart and bring them to my head, pull at the rope around my neck, it loosens and then I pull the cover off my head. I reached the surface and gasped for air. Sucking in all the air my lungs could hold. I notice three men, white men, on the edge of the bank. They are following me down the river. If they were to have any chance at catching me, they'll have to get in the water. It's at least semi rig length from bank to bank. I swam to the other side and reached for a tree limb, then pull myself to the bank. I heard a splash; I turn and look and one of the men had jumped in the water. I struggle to my feet and start a slow run. The rope is still hanging around my neck. Looking back, I see the man reach the center of the river. He's struggling in the river flow. It's obvious he doesn't swim much. Jaray, where's Jaray? I thought to myself, again.

"We're going to get you; you're not going to get out of here!" one man yelled out.

I continued running. Faster. Breathing in deep smooth breaths with every few steps. I reach to pull the rope off my neck. It hurt to the touch. The rope had burnt my skin, it had started to peel the skin off. A tree limb in front of me explodes, I run into some of its debris. I then hear a gunshot, then another. They are shooting at me from the other side of the river. I changed direction, not sure of what direction I was going in or where I was at. The rope loosened enough to where I could pull it off my neck. I let it drop to the ground. The only sound I heard now was my feet hitting the ground, twigs breaking under them. I tried to put as much distance as I could between me and them. I didn't know if they all came across the river or not, and I wasn't waiting to find out, either.

I came upon a field, someone's cattle pasture, a few cows grazing, one looked over at me and then continued grazing. The others never budged. The field turned back into woods. After I passed a few big trees, I stopped and hid behind one. Trying to settle my breath, I peeked around the tree to see if I could spot anyone. Nothing. I listen. Silence. My breathing is heavy but smooth. The perks of running from gang members in Harken. I started running again, more distance for them to travel if they wanted me so badly. The woods thickened some more, I had to slow down and fight through some vines, dead vines. I could see soda bottles and other trash debris laying around. Then a road.

On the road, I turned right. The local rivers flowed east to west, so I figured if I got out of the river on the north side then, my best bet would be to turn right. Going south! I should come upon a bridge soon. Now that I'm on the pavement, I know they'll never catch me on foot. They would have to be in a vehicle to catch up to me.

The road seemed to be curving. It curved to almost a complete circle, only there were woods on both sides of the road. It straightened out and I had realized where I was at. River Road. I live on River Road. It goes all the way north of my house and over the Saline River. I've never been out this far. If I keep going south, I should come up to my house. Those guys are probably not too far away from me now.

My running never pauses, every step, long. I could see a road coming up, a driveway, maybe. No, it's a road. It's Ferry Road. I've heard stories about that road. Maybe that's where they brought me. Yes. It makes sense. They took me out to Crain's Ferry. That's the area. It has to be. This means they are probably closer than I had anticipated. I have to get off this road. I duck into the woods on the east side of the road. I stop running and ease my way south, watching the road. Listening for any vehicles. I know I'm close to my house, maybe a mile away. If I could get there, I could call the police, call my unc, someone, anyone.

I hear a vehicle coming from the north. I pause. Watching closely. It's a pickup. Green. Three men in the cab. White men! That must be them. They are creeping, looking deeply into the woods on both sides. I'm down low enough, I don't think they can see me.

Why are they doing this to me? I thought to myself, what is it that they want to prove? That they can kill a black person, well, I'm white, too! I stay as still as possible. Letting them creep on by. I'll have a better chance of making it home if they leave the area. They keep driving. I rise up and start walking again, easing my way south, one tree at a time.

I could see that they sped up which told me they were by the houses. Which also told me I was close. I too, sped up. In just a few more minutes I would be home on the phone, trying to get a rescue. Up ahead I could see a clearing. The green truck was nowhere in sight. I get back on the road and started running up again. I could see my house and I noticed unc's car in my driveway. My first reaction was, relief, then I remembered Jaray drove unc's care to pick me up and we were hit. He could be still in the car.

When I reached the driveway, I could see that no one was in the car. There was a big dent on the back passenger-side. We were hit. I ran up on the porch and grabbed the knob. I didn't lock the door, or someone may have been in the house. Opening the door, I peeked inside. Saw the phone hanging on the wall by the kitchen door. I ran over to it and picked it up and dialed the police.

"Grayson Police Department!" Officer Stanley speaking.

"Officer Stanley, this is Ralphie Parsons…"

"Ralph, we've been looking for you!"

"We who?"

"The police department and your Aunty Janie and Uncle Ronnie. Your mother and Jaray were in car accidents and are at the hospital."

"Both of them, how are they? Are they okay?"

"Well, I'm not sure. Yes, the both of them are at the hospital. Jaray must have been looking for you to tell you about your mother and backed out into traffic leaving your house."

"No. I was with Jaray when he backed out into the road. Then everything went dark. The next thing I know I was laying tied up, my head covered and a rope around my neck," I said, remembering Jaray telling me about my mother, "And I guess the limb broke or something and I fell into the river. I was able to swim across the river and get away, but they are looking for me, they are in a green pickup truck. Can someone come to my house and pick me up?"

"Okay, Ralph, I'm on my way now!" Officer Stanley said. "Stay in your house and away from any windows. Lock the doors. I'm on my way!"

He hung up the phone. I paused then dialed unc's number.

Ring.

Ring.

Ring. Ring. Ring. Ring.

No answer yet, they are not home. I peeked through the curtain out into the street. Didn't see anyone. No green truck. No police. I backed away. Picked up the phone, grabbed the phone book. Looked up the number to the hospital. Found the number and dialed it.

Ring.

Ring.

Ring.

"Grayson Memorial, how may I direct your call?"

"Uh, I'm trying to reach Janie Morre or Ronnie Morre. Are they there? My mother and cousin are in the hospital. Barbara Morre and Jaray Morre."

"Yes, hold please."

Ring. Ring.

"Hello!"

"Unc! How's my mother?"

"Ralphie, where are you? Where have you been?"

"It's Ralphie!" he whispered to Aunty Janie as if she didn't hear him just say my name!

"Your mother is unconscious right now, Ralphie, you need to get here!" unc said.

"Unconscious, is she going to be okay?" I swallowed.

"I'm not sure, doc is waiting on results from CT."

I took a breath and said, "I'm at home right now, it's a long story. Officer Stanley is on his way to pick me up. Someone is trying to kill me. They ran into your car when Jaray and I were…"

Knock. Knock.

"Ralphie? It's Officer Stanley!"

"Officer Stanley is here. He is going to bring me to the hospital, okay. I'll see you in a minute!"

"Okay. Bye!"

I hung up as Officer Stanley was coming in through the front door.

"Ralphie?"

"I'm here," I say, coming around the door. His gun half out of the holster. He peered down at me.

"Come on. Let's get you to the hospital, you look terrible kid."

"I'm okay, my neck and head are sore, and my eyes feel like they were just put back in their sockets."

He opens the passenger door of his patrol car and lets me get in and shuts the door. He goes around the front of the car and makes his way to the driver side, he is looking down at the road, then opens the door and gets in. My mind raced. He put the car into gear and began driving.

"I want to get a statement from you when we get to the hospital. I know you want to go in and see your mother and cousin first, but I do need that statement. That way we can try and find who did this to you!" Officer Stanley said, putting on his blinker and pulling onto Main street.

"Okay!"

"You said green truck?

"Yes, sir, white rims!"

"No license plate number?"

"Didn't think about that! Three white men. They had guns, too. They shot at me, tried to hang me!"

"Okay, anything else?"

"They took me out to Crain's Ferry."

He pulled into the hospital emergency parking. Parked. Pulled out a legal pad and began writing on it.

"Was it down Ferry Road?"

"Yes, I think so. I went across the river and I ran. I ran into a field then back into more woods. Then I found a paved road. I recognized it, but not at first because it curved fairly good before straightening out. That's when I had realized it was River Road. I ran, then ducked into the woods because I'd realized they took me to Crain's Ferry. While in the woods I'd heard a vehicle, and it was the green pickup truck with three white men. They drove by slowly, looking on both sides of the road. Then they sped off. I noticed the houses and got back on the road and ran to my house and called you."

"You did good, kid!" he said, putting away the legal pad. "That'll be good for now, go in and see your mother!"

"Okay!" I opened the door, climbed out of the patrol car, and headed for the front door. I spotted the green pickup driving by.

"That's them!" I yelled at Officer Stanley, "That's the truck!" My heart raced as I yelled. My voice gave my fear away.

He turned and looked, turned on the lights and siren, and began pursuit of the green truck! The driver of the truck punched on the gas and sped away, quickly. There was nothing more I could do so I walked into the hospital.

"Aunty Janie! Which room is my mother in?" I asked as I spotted Aunty Janie coming down the corridor!

"Oh my, Ralphie, are you okay?"

"Yes. I'll be fine," I said, feeling my neck. "Which room?"

"She's in 101. I'll be right there; I'm getting something to drink for your uncle. Do you want anything?"

"Yes, please," I said, turning, looking at the room numbers as I walked down the corridor. I spotted the room and on the left. I opened the door and saw unc sitting on the chair next to my mother. He saw me and got up to greet me.

"Ralphie!" he said, standing now.

"I'm okay, unc. How's mom?"

"It's not looking good, Ralphie!"

# CHAPTER 6

# GOD WORKS MIRACLES

The tears in my already swollen eyes stood at attention. I stared down at my mother, her face barely visible through all the bandaging. Her body was covered with blankets up to her neck. I put my hand down to touch hers through the blanket. She never moved; she didn't even know I was here.

"Doctors say they don't have the results yet, it's possibly a coma!" unc says, rubbing my shoulder then putting his arm around me. Standing next to me in a place a father should be, "I'm sorry, Ralph, I wish things were different."

"Different how?" Tears fell down my face. "Different, like I wasn't a biracial kid, half black? Take a look around unc, those racist pricks are trying to kill me and here I am standing next to my mother, she's lying here, and we don't know if she will make it or not. Who knows what happened out there, was it even in an accident? Jaray's here in the hospital, too, and it just so happens, he's biracial as well. It doesn't seem like a coincidence to me, unc, it seems planned!"

Unc stood there in silence. More tears fell down my face. I knew I had to be right about us being targeted, and deep down, I think unc knew it as well.

Aunty Janie came in with our drinks. She handed unc his, then stood beside me, two more drinks in her hands. She stared down at my mother, holding her tears back, being strong for all of us. She attempted to hand me my drink, I stood there, tears had already paused. I grabbed the drink but didn't get a drink right away. Staring at my mother. I closed my eyes, thinking I'm going to get those bastards for what they did to us.

"How's Jaray?" I asked Aunty Janie while opening my drink and taking a sip.

"He's doing okay, still asleep! He hit his head on the driver's side window. It broke the glass and cut up the left side of his face a good amount. Seventeen stitches. They say he'll need…"

"Mr. and Mrs. Morre. Jaray is awake!" a nurse said, mispronouncing his name as Jay-ray, instead of Jah-ray. She came in the room, taking a moment to check on my mother, then looked over at me, "Oh wow, are you okay? You may need to see Doctor Reed!"

"I'm okay!" I said, feeling my neck again. People looking at my neck may be a normal thing now.

The nurse looked over at Aunty Janie, pointing at me saying, "He needs to see the doctor!"

"Okay, I'll make sure of it, thank you!" Aunt Janie replies.

"I'm going to go talk to Jaray, which room is he in?" I asked unc, who had already sat back down and was drinking his bottled soda. Aunty Janie was still standing beside me staring at my mother. They were once best friends, long ago, when they were kids. A friendship grown apart by distance and age.

"Go ahead, he's in Room 112, just down the hall, I will be down in a minute." Aunty Janie said, without removing her eyes from my mother. Unc in a daze, eyes staring at nothing in front of him. He did shake his head, though, but I don't think it had anything to do with what I had asked him. I turned and looked down at my mother again. Thinking it's possible that this could be the last time I will see her alive. We just didn't know anything yet. I didn't want to leave and knew if I did something would happen. Those bastards, I thought to myself. I stood next to my mother and cried some more. Tears falling like rain. The nurse left us. I heard her say in a whisper as she walked out the door, "Excuse me."

Knock. Knock.

I turned and looked, my face shining in the light from the tears wetting my cheeks. It was Jaray standing in the doorway. "How is she? What happened?" he asked, slowly walking in, his gown fit loosely around him. He never liked anything tight around his waist. The left side of his face was bandaged and looked like a mask. He made his way to unc, who broke out of his daze and stood up to help Jaray sit where he was sitting.

"It's not looking good, Jaray!" unc answered. "Doc says she may be in a coma, not sure yet!" Jaray turned and looked at me, his eyes saying everything he couldn't voice. Tears streamed down the right side of his face, the bandages caught the tears on the left, soaking them up. His eyes left me and went to my mother. I followed his eyes and looked at her, too. My mother. My friend. Would possibly never know what happened to her, or what happened to me.

Thinking back to the last time I talked with her. I was about to leave for church. She was taking pictures of me, so happy that I was going to church. A mother very proud of her kid. Then it dawned on me and I blurted out, "What was she doing at work on a Sunday?"

Everyone looked at me. Pondering the question, I looked at Aunty Janie, "You knew she was at work, you said you'd call her at work and have her come down to the police station. Why was she at work?"

"She had come to the store this morning to fill her car up with gas, she said she was called to go in and prepare for a Monday meeting because there was a big meeting coming up between the mining company lawyers and executives. It's probably about Mr. Evanson, he is on his deathbed and owns the majority of the company. I called her and told her what was going on and she said she'd meet y'all at the police station. On her way, though, she must have run off the road."

"Someone did call the police to report an accident on twenty-seven by mile marker eighteen. After receiving the call, Officer Madison let all of us go and headed to the scene." I said, remembering the phone call Officer Madison received, "I think someone may have run her off the road!"

"That has to be it because someone smashed into unc's car," Jaray started, remembering what happened earlier that put him in the hospital. "Ralphie, they hit you with a tire iron or something, and took you out of the car..." he paused and put his hand on his head, the pain of it was all coming back to him. "They took you out of the car and then another man jumped in the passenger seat and smashed my head against the window, that's all I remember. Is that what they did to you?" he asked pointing at my neck.

Aunty and unc's faces looked stunned. They looked at each other then looked at my neck again. Puzzled.

"A paramedic heading to his shift in Dallas came upon your uncle's car in the middle of the street. He noticed you inside and got out to help. He said it looked like it may have been a hit and run, which, in a way, I guess it was. He checked on you and pulled you out and rushed you here to the hospital. I heard him say a car accident on River Road and I immediately ran over to see who it was, and it was you," Aunty Janie said. She has always been a nosy rosy!

"Ralphie, I'm glad to see that you're okay, although, you look worse than I feel! What happened?" Jaray asked, looking at my neck.

I told them that I remembered waking up and feeling something around my neck. My hands taped behind my back. My head covered. "They tried to hang me, the limb broke or something and I fell in the water at the Saline River. I was able to get away from them, three white men in a green pickup, possibly the KKK."

"Make sense to me!" Jaray said.

Unc spoke up and said, "No, it can't be the KKK. That group hasn't been here since the early 1950s when this was what they called a sundown town."

"Well, they sure acted like the Klan to me!" I said, feeling around my neck at the rope burns. "Officer Stanley took off after the green truck when he dropped me off outside. I saw the truck driving by before I came inside and told Officer Stanley!"

"What are we going to do, unc?" Jaray asked.

"Boys, we know there is obviously something amiss going on here, and I'm not sure if it's all tied together, although, it sure as hell looks like it just might be. As for the KKK, I don't know. We, or, you boys, are probably safer here in the hospital than anywhere else. I'll go and talk to the officers and see what they have found out," unc said, looking over at my mother. He too, knew this could be the last time he would see her alive, laying there breathing, not moving, not speaking.

We all looked at each other and then at my mother, laying on her hospital bed, breathing normally as if she were only asleep and would wake up any moment. Maybe a coma kept her asleep, maybe not, but either way, she was away from the dangers that life has in store for the rest of us. Watching my mother who may be on her deathbed and there being nothing I could do about it, it really hurt inside. Tears kept falling from all our faces, my nose running, my neck and head in pain. I stood there, there is no other place I would rather be.

"May I come in?" Pastor Mike asked, knocking on the door, breaking the silence in the room.

"Please," unc said.

"I just heard what happened and thought I'd come down and show my support. Anything I can do for any of you?"

We all looked at each other, shook our heads to say no.

"Maybe a prayer!" I spoke up after thinking a moment.

"Yes, that would be wonderful!" Aunt Janie agreed.

"Okay, perfect. God only knows what we need," Pastor Mike said, coming closer to the bed.

"Father, we come to you in dire need. A mother lays here, patiently waiting for your word. Her family surrounds her, with love, compassion, and they want to see your will be done. I ask that you send your lovely angels to comfort them in their time of need. Give them strength, Lord, the strength needed to deal with the here and now and the strength to deal with the things to come. Only you know what we all need, individually, and together. A family found only in your love. The love you dish out to us every moment of our lives. Come closer to us as we come closer to you, in prayer, in Jesus name, amen."

"Amen," unc said, patting Pastor Mike on the shoulder. Pastor Mike looked over at him and patted him on the back in return.

"Amen. Lord, bring us a miracle!" Aunty Janie added.

"Let me know if you need anything, anything at all," Pastor Mike said, looking around the room at everyone. "Ronnie, could I talk to you a moment, outside?"

"Yeah, sure!" unc said then looked over at aunty as to say he'll be right back.

They both stepped out. Jaray silently rubbed his head feeling the bandages on his face. The pain he obviously felt hidden behind the same bandages. Aunty Janie standing beside the bed, her pain showing in her face, the sadness so deep, it may never find its way out. Here I am, ripped and torn, probably needing the doctor as the nurse suggested, my skin color is probably what brought all this on us. I shake my head in disgust. Anger building up inside me. My grandmother came to mind, if only to calm me. Anger is a foothold for the devil, she would say.

"Jaray!"

I looked over at my mother! Could it be?

"Jaray!"

It was. She was calling for Jaray! I raced over to her bedside, bumping Aunty Janie, who was already bending down, comforting my mother.

"We are here, Barb!"

"Mom!"

Jaray makes his way to the other side of her bed. She looks at all of us, one by one and stops at Jaray.

"You're alive!" she says, her voice shaky.

She looked more stunned about Jaray being alive than we are about her. She had just woken up and the doctors didn't even have the results back yet. She hadn't responded to anything, so the doctor thought she didn't have any brain activity and had ordered a CAT scan. Now, here she is talking and looking at us. God works miracles.

Aunty Janie grabbed the pillow speaker and pushed the nurse call button to call the nurse. My mother pulled her arms out from under the blankets, reaching for me. I wiped my tears and embraced her reach.

"My baby," she said, hugging me tightly.

The nurse came walking in and silenced the nurse call and walked over to my mother's bed, "It's a miracle! I have to call Doctor Reed!" She checked my mother's vitals and after checking the IV machine, she walked out of the room.

My mother was not dead, but awake and talking. She must have heard us talking about Jaray being cared for in the hospital, too. I once read that people could sometimes hear what is going on around them when they're unconscious or in a coma. I watched my mother; she would appear asleep then she was awake again.

"Mom, squeeze my hand!" I said when she would close her eyes, my heart racing. She would squeeze and I would feel relieved. Her going in and out terrified me. I thought of the worst.

Doctor Reed walked in, "I hear we have a miracle. Let me check some things out. It's not every day we have someone come around so quickly. My mother looked at him and he at her as he grabbed her hand, "Mrs. Morre, how are you feeling?"

"Ms. Morre. Not Mrs!" she corrected. "I'm a little hoarse and I feel like I have a sore throat."

"That's probably from the endotracheal tube that was placed in your trachea on your transport here to the hospital. Let me take a look at your throat, say ahh!" He leaned in and shined a small flashlight into her throat! He then put it away and continued, "They found you hunched over your vehicle's console, it appeared you had hit your head on the steering wheel, probably several times, your seat belt had choked you and constricted your breathing. After the EMS brought you in, we administered medications to elevate your blood pressure and placed you on a ventilator to support your breathing and IV fluids for hydration, all of which were to support the brain to help it to recover from injury. You showed no sign of improvement. However, we were able to stabilize your breathing, that was all we were able to do, though. Your vital organs were not injured. You didn't move spontaneously.

When blood was drawn from your left arm, you didn't even wince. It appears you had sustained severe brain damage that caused severely impaired consciousness. A coma. We'll need to do some more tests to..."

Unc walks in and sees Doctor Reed. He thinks the worst at first, but then looks down at my mother and seen her eyes open. "Barbara, you're conscious! Oh God, thank you!" He made his way over to her and leaned in for a hug, she raised her hands to embrace him.

"Barb, what happened?"

My mother took a deep breath, released unc, and just as she was about to tell him, Aunty Janie said, "She'll have plenty of time to tell us, Ronnie."

"No, it's okay, everyone needs to hear this," my mother said, pausing enough to look around the room. "After I received the call from you, Janie, I left to get to the police station for Ralphie. I didn't want them accusing him of anything, you know how this city can get sometimes. As soon as I hit twenty-seven, I had noticed a red suburban behind me. I remember seeing the same suburban parked in the parking lot at work. I thought they were just leaving, too, but then they came up beside me honking and smashed into the side of my car, forcing me to fight to stay on the road. They backed off and then came up again, only hitting me from behind this time. I pressed down on the gas pedal to try and outrun them.

That's when they sped up beside me again and hit me in the rear driver's side forcing the car to flip. I'm not sure how many times. I don't remember anything after the car first flipped. That must have been when I hit my head."

Doctor Reed excused himself after his pager went off. Unc sat up and said, "I'm glad you're not in a coma. There has been a lot going on, I just talked with Pastor Mike and he said E.W. is dropping the charges on the windshield being broken out of his car."

"The windshield?" my mother said, puzzled.

"We didn't break his window!" I said, "That is a lie, Daron spit on his windshield, that's all that was done!"

"It doesn't matter, now, no charges are being filed," Uncle Ronnie said, again.

"Why was he lying anyway?" I asked, standing up from the side of the bed where I had been sitting "He started in on me while we were looking around reading stuff at the Salt Palace, so I left the building and Daron and Jarod stayed there a few minutes longer before coming out in a hurry. They said he called us names, probably nigger and nigger lover! Daron spat on the windshield and then we all took off running because the guy came out. That's the truth. Maybe he was so mad about it he tried to kill me out there at Crain's Ferry."

"I'm not sure, however, Pastor Mike said the police picked up E.W. and he was dropping the charges on the windshield."

"What did they pick him up for?" I asked.

"I don't know!"

A knock on the door grabbed everyone's attention, "I heard you were in here," Ed Setsmen said. "I wanted to check on you, I'm here checking on Mr. Evanson, he's down the hall!"

"Ed, thank you. How'd the meeting go?" my mother asked.

"Barb, the meeting is tomorrow morning."

"Oh, I'm sorry, I don't know how long I've been in here."

"It's okay, I hope you get better soon, we'll be okay without you, you take all the time you need, okay!"

"Thank you, but I do have a question for you."

"Sure!"

"Who drives the red suburban?"

The look in Ed's eye says he knew who drove the suburban, he tried to hide the look and said, "I'm not sure there is anyone who drives a red suburban, Barb. Why?"

"Because they ran me off the road, Ed!"

"I'm sorry, please get some rest. I'll see you later," Ed said, turning and walking out of the door.

"Who else saw what I saw in Ed's eyes and face?" Jaray asked, looking at everyone in the room. "Seems like he knows more than he is letting on."

"Yes, I saw that, too!" Aunty Janie agreed.

"What did we see?" Doctor Reed asked, entering the room.

"Oh, nothing," Aunt Janie replied.

"I'm here to check on the boy, my nurse says he needed some attention, so I came to check him out."

"Yes, Ralphie, go with Doctor Reed," Aunty Janie says, lightly patting my back while guiding me toward Dr. Reed.

"Ralphie, my Nurse Amy will take you down to triage. I'll be there in a moment; I want to look over some things with Ms. Morre here."

"Okay, mom, I'll be right back."

"You go, Ralphie, I'll be okay."

I walked with the nurse down the hall to the triage room. She opens the door and allows me to enter first. I make my way to the exam table and sit down. It was cold. I could feel goosebumps on my knees as the cool air from the vents above blew through the rips in my khaki pants.

"Let me check some vitals, left or right arm?" Nurse Amy asks, holding a blood pressure cuff.

"Does it matter which one?"

"No, not at all!"

She placed the cuff on my right arm, filled it with air.

While waiting on the results, Doctor Reed entered the room, "Wow, Amy, this room is freezing!" Looking at the thermostat strategically placed by the door, he turned the temperature up. "Dang thing is set at fifty degrees. There that should get it warmed up. I'm going to have to talk with maintenance about this!"

He makes his way over to the exam table as Nurse Amy was removing the blood pressure cuff, "What happened to you, Ralphie?"

"It's a long story, I have to make an official police report when Officer Stanley gets back."

"Well, you're in luck, because I just saw him coming in the front before I came in here."

"Good."

"I'm glad your mother came out okay, I really wasn't expecting that at all. Some people don't recover, but it seems God has other plans. She really is a fighter, your mother!" Doctor Reed said, checking the rope burns around my neck. "Nurse Amy, would you go and get Officer Stanley, so that he and Ralphie could talk. I'll treat and bandage this up really quick and you will be ready to talk to the officer."

"Sure, doc," Nurse Amy says, walking out closing the door behind her.

"Ralphie, whatever happened, it looks like you're going to be fine but may have some permanent scarring around the neck. Say ahh!" I open my mouth to do what he said, he checked my throat and patted my shoulder, "Looks good!"

"Yeah, I figured that. It hurt like crazy pulling the rope off, though," I said as there was a knock on the door.

Nurse Amy came back in and asked, "Would you like Officer Stanley to come in?"

"That would be fine!"

"Yeah, that'll be fine, I'm wrapping up now. Pun intended!" Doctor Reed said, finishing the wrap on my neck.

"Okay, I'll send him in!"

"Ralphie, you take care of this, you hear, I'll send some cream home with you and it should heal up within a week, a little scaring is possible."

"Okay, great!"

"Doctor Reed, how are you?" Officer Stanley said, "Ralphie?" he then tipped his head to me.

"Officer Stanley, you better get whoever did this to Ralphie and get them quick," Doctor Reed demanded.

"Well, we already have one perp!"

"Good!"

"You caught one of those bastards?" I asked, half shocked. I knew he was already in pursuit after he had dropped me off here.

"Yeah, we caught the driver of the green pickup! Officer Madison is still interrogating at the station as we speak."

"Gentleman, I have to check on other patients, I'll excuse myself. Ralphie, take care of those wounds, okay?"

"I will, thanks!"

"The driver of the green pickup was E.W. Johns; he was with two other individuals, earlier. He claims he was being held at gunpoint but with the other incident earlier today, we think it was connected. He was upset because you guys broke his windshield…"

"We did not break his windshield!" I interrupted.

"I believe you and that's why there are no charges being written on you boys. There is no reason to try and kill someone over a broken windshield. He hasn't come clean just yet but with your report, we may be able to get the names of the other two involved. Did you get a look at any of them?"

"No, they had a bag or something over my head and when I was able to get the bag off, I was too busy trying to get away from them to see who they were or what they even looked like."

"Well, we know a couple of fellers that run with E.W. and they may be the ones involved but without any evidence, we cannot move on them just yet. Is there anything else you remember that may help the case in any way?"

"No sir, green truck, three white guys. That's about all I can give you!"

# CHAPTER 7

# THE FBI

Officer Stanley walked with me back down to my mother's room, we both walked inside. Officer Stanley greeted everyone. Told my mother they were working on getting those involved with trying to kill me. Unc turned to Officer Stanley and said, "Someone in a red suburban ran Barb off the road."

"A red suburban?" Officer Stanley asked.

"Yes, you know who that may be?" unc questioned.

"I'll run a few things when I get back to the station, and I'll make a report for you Barb. It has started to seem to me that this all may be connected. I must go and speak with Officer Madison, so I'll be in touch!"

When Officer Stanley left the room, everyone went quiet. My mother broke the silence with a joke, "Ralphie, that's a nice necklace you have there," talking about the bandages Doctor Reed just put on the wound.

We all woke the room with laughter, but the pain was still real. "Yeah, well your headband is just as nice!"

During our laughs, my mother said she needed to go to the restroom, Aunty Janie came over to the bed to help her.

"I can't move my legs!"

"You can't?" Aunty Janie asked, then said, "Let's call the nurse." She pushed the nurse call button. My heart began pounding, I was afraid there was something majorly wrong and she would never be the same.

Doctor Reed and Nurse Amy came into the room, Nurse Amy silenced the nurse call and Doctor Reed walked to my mother, "Is everything okay?" he asked, looking her over.

"I can't move my legs!" my mother says.

"Hmm...that happens in some cases, let's try something." He pulls the blanket away from her legs, exposing her feet and shins. He then runs a pen-like device over her feet and then up her shins. "Do you feel that?"

"Yes!"

"Try and move your legs."

"Okay." She tried to move both legs, "No, I can't!"

"Okay, you may have paresis of the legs. Which is a condition of muscular weakness caused by nerve damage, which could have happened from a brain injury. We could check the peripheral nerve. Let me order some labs and MRI."

"Okay, thank you, doctor."

Nurse Amy and Doctor Reed left the room. Unc stood up, "You boys want to go to the house to get some rest?" he asked.

"Yes!" Jaray answered.

I was a little hesitant and looked at my mother, she tilted her and said, "Go ahead Ralphie. The doctor is ordering some labs and MRI, so I'll be busy doing that. Not to worry, though, everything is in God's hands."

\*\*\*

When we made it to unc's house, he said I could sleep in the guest room. I went into the room and shut the door. I was tired and worried about my mother. I did fall asleep and the next thing I knew, Jaray was waking me up, "Your mom is being released from the hospital and is coming to here and to stay for a little while. The doctor said she would probably be in a wheelchair for a while, but he set up physical therapy for her. She should get to walk again as her body heals." I was relieved to hear that she would possibly walk and was relieved to hear she was coming. Jaray said, "Aunty Janie is bringing her here within the hour."

I hadn't realized that I slept for ten hours. It was Monday morning, and I couldn't remember the last time I had something to eat.

"I'm hungry!" I said to Jaray.

"Well, you're in luck because unc just went and picked up some food from Micky D's. Now get up and let's eat."

"I'm up!"

I went into the bathroom and splashed some water on my face. Looked at myself in the mirror. I didn't have a toothbrush so brushing my teeth was out of the question.

"Ralphie!" unc yells.

"I'm coming, unc!"

"Officer Madison is here and needs to speak with us!"

"Okay!" I make my way to the living room and to see Officer Madison and Officer Stanley standing by the front door.

"Did you find them the rest of those bastards?" I asked.

"No. We haven't found them, but we know who they are. We've found out that they are working for someone, though, someone from Evanson's Salt Company. They were hired to kill, these are their words, not ours, but they were hired to kill the black boy that lives with the white lady! Which, to them it is you," Officer Madison said.

"Why?" I was stunned. "What did I do to them? Or is it because I am black?"

"It could well be; however, E.W. says it has nothing to do with your skin color. They were told to make it look like it was, though." Officer Madison said.

"Yeah, so they did what they thought the Klan would do," Officer Stanley began saying, "They probably started with the Klan newspaper."

"Would make sense. We found one in our front yard!"

"Yes, that's what Pastor Mike said. You mentioned to Daron and Jarod that you found a Klan paper in your yard a few days ago."

"Yeah. Are the guys you're looking for members of the KKK?" I asked.

"No. Just some local boys who think they are! Their family was once a part of the branch that was here in the late 1920s through the 1950s and they run around acting like they are the KKK!" Officer Madison said.

"What I do not understand, though, is why someone from Evanson's Salt would want Ralphie or Barb dead?" unc asked the officers. "What is going on over there? I know that Mr.

Evanson is in the hospital and probably will be dying soon, but why is someone trying to kill Barb and Ralphie? It just doesn't make any sense."

"That's what we are investigating. We have to call in the FBI because it appears to be a hate crime, even if E.W. says it's not." Officer Madison said looking at unc then down at his pager, which was buzzing on his belt.

"Officer Stanley and I will have to get going, you guys be careful and try to stay out of sight for a little while. I'll have an officer parked outside here and at the hospital until further notice."

"Barb is being released and Janie is bringing her here within the hour," unc said.

"Okay, we will have the officer escort them here!" Officer Madison said. "We should get going, please be careful!"

"Thanks, gentlemen," unc said, walking the officers out the door.

"That does not make any sense, unc! Why would anyone from Evanson's Salt Company want us dead? We don't have anything to do with the salt company except for my mother doing secretary work."

"Yeah, I feel ya. It doesn't make sense to me either," Jaray says.

"Well boys, it may just be a hate thing. These boys are acting like that because of your skin color."

"Unc. You know it has to be," Jaray said. "They just want to put the blame on someone else."

Unc shook his head in agreement and started walking to the kitchen, "Let's go eat boys." Jaray and I followed behind him and made our way to the kitchen bar. We sat down, grabbed a bacon, egg, and cheese biscuit. Unc poured himself another cup of coffee and reached into the refrigerator and grabbed the orange juice, then pulled two glasses from the cabinet and set them in front of us. "Pour you guys some orange juice."

"Thanks, unc!" I said, my mind still on why they were trying to kill me and my mother. She just started working for Evanson's Salt Company, so I was sure no one really knew her, and I didn't break any windshields, so this all had to be because of the color of my skin. Officer Madison said E.W. told him that someone hired them to kill me and probably someone to run my mother off the road to kill her.

"Ralphie, snap out of it!" Jaray said, snapping his fingers in front of my face.

"Sorry, I just can't make any sense of why they want us dead!"

"I know, I cannot figure anything out either, unc, any ideas?"

Unc shakes his head to acknowledge that he didn't, he only spoke when he swallowed some of his breakfast biscuit and looked at me, "Not really. Just maybe it has something to do with Mr. Evanson on his deathbed, and maybe your mother saw or heard something she shouldn't have during their meeting yesterday."

"Yeah, maybe so!"

"Ron! Ronnie!" Aunty Janie yelled from the living room, "Come and help me with Barb!"

We all got up from the bar and headed toward the living room, Aunty Janie put down her keys and turned to go back out to the driveway where my mother was waiting in the car. The officer parked out front was getting out of his car to assist. Between unc, Aunty Janie, and the officer, they got my mother into her wheelchair and brought her into the house. Luckily unc and aunty's front door was level with the ground so bringing her in wasn't much of a problem.

They wheeled my mother into the kitchen, and I offered her one of the bacon, egg and cheese biscuits, which she refused. "Just give me some water please, and a cup of coffee would be nice, too. The coffee at the hospital wasn't so great."

"Coming right up!" Aunt Janie said, pulling the coffee pot out and reaching for a coffee cup in the cabinet. I reached in the refrigerator for one of the bottled waters and handed it to my mother.

"Thanks, Ralphie, did you get any sleep last night?"

"Yes, ma'am! I slept the whole entire night."

"Good, I'm glad you did. We've been through a lot!"

"Have you heard what the officers said?"

"Yes, they stopped by this morning and told me, and they said they would come by and talk to your uncle!"

"They didn't tell me who their suspects were but that the FBI is probably being brought in because they are ruling it a hate crime," my mother said, Aunty Janie, handing her the cup of coffee she poured. No sugar, black.

"How long is that going to take? I don't want to be just sitting around here all the time. You know I don't like to sit around unless I'm reading and unc and aunty don't have any books around here," I said.

My mother, looking at unc and aunty, smiled softly and shook her head.

"Maybe your Uncle Ronnie or Aunt Janie could go to the house and get your book?" mom said.

"That would be great, I'm almost done with it, they could take me to the library, too!"

\*\*\*

We stayed with unc and aunty for the next two weeks waiting on the FBI and police to get back to us. We never left the house, if we needed anything aunty or unc would go and get it. It was kind of nice, even though I didn't have much to read after finishing *Killing Floor,* but I'd spent most of my time in Jaray's room listening to music and playing his PlayStation.

\*\*\*

I started eating my breakfast unc had picked up from McDonald's again and the phone rang. Unc reached over the counter and picked up the phone from the wall. "Hello!"

"Yes, this is him!" He looked over at my mother. "Yes, she is here!" He started shaking his head no like they could see him doing so. "No, I think it would be best if you guys came here. She's only been out of the hospital for a couple of weeks and is currently in a wheelchair!" He then began shaking his head yes. "Okay, we'll see you then."

He hung up the phone and said, "That was FBI Agent Benson, he and his partner, I forget his name, are here from Dallas and wanted Barb to come to the police station. I told them it would be better for them to come here. So, they'll be over in thirty minutes."

"Wow, the actual FBI!" I said, taking another bite of my breakfast biscuit.

Unc, Jaray, and I sat at the bar, and my mother and Aunt Janie sat around the kitchen table, the room went silent. My mother sipped her coffee, Aunt Janie did the same. Jaray finished his breakfast, stood, and started downing his orange juice. Unc stared off into space, deep in thought. I looked at unc, he seemed restless. I'm not so sure he slept at all last night. He has been the go-to in the family since my grandfather passed a few years ago. He has taken in Jaray even though his kids were grown and living by Dallas. Jaray's mother would only come by when she wanted some money, unc would give in, even though he knew she would buy alcohol. Aunty Janie would throw a fit because he gave her money. Jaray got to where he didn't really think his mother would ever stop drinking. He loved her but didn't like her drinking and didn't want to be around her when she was. My grandfather wouldn't give her any money, he'd make her sober up first. Unc would just give her money and tell her to sober up, which she only would after she spent the money on booze. He needed to rest.

"Unc, you didn't sleep last night, did you?" I asked. Mom and Aunty Janie looked over at me then at unc.

"Not really."

"Ron!" Aunty Janie said. "You need to rest. You don't need to have another issue with your heart!"

"I know Janie! It's just that there is a lot going on right now! I'll rest later after the FBI comes by, okay?"

"You better!"

Jaray had left the kitchen and mumbled something about a shower. Moments later we could hear the shower running in the bathroom. Jaray always took a shower, sometimes twice a day. It depended on what he was doing. I guess the breakfast crumbs got on him or something, who knows? His showers would last for like an hour or so.

"I could use one of those," my mother said, talking about the shower we heard running.

"Yeah, me too. I'll help you when Jaray gets out, it may be a while though," Aunty Janie said.

"Oh yeah, I know, Jaray and his showers!" My mother said and everyone cracked up laughing.

Aunty Janie got up from the kitchen table and started cleaning the dishes. She never liked to have dirty dishes. One time, during one of our trips here from Harken to visit, I would pick on Aunty Janie and lick her plates. She would wash and wash and I thought she was going to beat the crap out of me. It was all in fun and she always had a good sense of humor.

I thought about licking some plates just to aggravate her but didn't.

Unc went into the living room and I heard the television turn on and a sports announcer talking about the Sunday night baseball game. Detroit Tigers versus Texas Rangers at the ballpark in Arlington. The Rangers won seven to six. I think he was just trying to drown out his thoughts. He would do that at times, especially when other people were here. Almost every time we had family get-togethers, unc would be glued to the television. My grandfather would do the same thing.

Aunty finished up the dishes and went and knocked on the bathroom door. "What is it?" Jaray asked.

"Jaray, hurry up, your Aunt Barb wants to get cleaned up."

"Okay, I've got to shampoo my hair!"

"What have you been doing in there this whole time?"

"Washing my beautiful body, ha-ha!"

"Well, hurry up!"

"Okay!"

"Ron, turn that television down, please. You're going to wake the neighborhood!"

"Well, they should have been up by now anyway!" unc said, reaching for the remote to turn the volume down.

My mother and I are still in the kitchen, listening to everyone else. "Ralphie, are you sure you're okay? You've been a quiet lately!"

"Yeah, I just don't know what to think at this moment. The gangs back in Harken never tried to kill me, they would just jump me and beat me up warn me not to come around their neighborhood. No one ever called the FBI, that's a hate crime, too. They would hate the colors I wore and beat me up because of it. No FBI, ever!"

"I know honey, it's not the same, though!"

"No, but it is the same, mom! They tried to kill me because the skin I wear is black!"

"Yeah, but they hate you because of what you are. The gangs just didn't like what you were wearing. The difference is you can take the clothes off, but not your skin color!"

"It's just ridiculous, mom! All of it. The gangs, the KKK. It's stupid!"

"Well, Satan uses things like that to separate people."

"Satan sucks!" I said, then leaned over to my mother and kissed her on the cheek. "I'm ready to go home."

"Well, we can go home after the FBI comes by to talk to us. I'll have Janie take us home, well, at least after I get cleaned up!"

"Okay, mom!"

Aunty Janie walks in and overhears us talking about going home. "Are you sure you want to do that, Barb? There is no problem with you two staying here as long as you need to."

"I just think that us being home will help us both feel better!" my mother said, rubbing my back.

"Okay then, after Jaray gets his clean butt out of the shower and we let the water heat back up, because you know he used every bit of it. We'll get you cleaned up and take you home."

My mother thanked Aunty Janie and we heard the television go silent, maybe unc turned it off.

Knock. Knock.

"Must be the agents," Aunty Janie said, rising up from the kitchen table heading into the living room.

"Hey, Mr. Morre! We spoke on the phone! I'm Agent Kevin Benson and this is my partner, Joe Vitrees." The agents showed their badges to unc as Aunty Janie came up behind him.

"You guys come in and have a seat. Would you like anything to drink?" Aunty Janie asks them. "I'll go get Barb and Ralphie!"

"We're coming Aunty Janie."

"No, we're okay!" The agents said as they walked in the door. They walked over to the couch and were about to take a seat when I wheeled my mother through the door. They paused for a moment and then sat. Jaray came around the corner and stopped, a towel wrapped around his waist, loosely.

"Oops!" he said, then turned around and went to his room. Everyone started laughing, including the FBI agents.

"Sorry, he's just too comfortable in his nakedness," Aunty Janie said, still laughing.

"It's okay, we'll try and forget about that. Let's get down to business, shall we?" Agent Benson said.

# CHAPTER 8

# A FAMILIAR VOICE

"Tell us everything you think is related to the case and Agent Vitrees and I will investigate until we get to the bottom of it."

"Well, let Ralphie tell his part. What happened to him while I was in the hospital."

"Okay, Ralphie, go ahead!" Agent Benson said, looking over at me, his notepad and pen in hand, ready to take notes.

"Didn't Officer Madison and Stanley tell you what happened?" I asked.

"Yes, but sometimes stories get a little twisted. Agent Vitrees and I would like to hear firsthand."

"Okay, fine. I understand," I paused and took several breaths. "Going through everything that happened that Sunday in my head. Leaving for the church, listening to Pastor

Mike preach about us being salt of the earth. After church, going to the Salt Palace. Having a confrontation with E.W. and Daron spitting on E.W.'s car. Eating lunch at Jared's grandmother's house. Walking around and stopping at the store where Officer Madison and Pastor Mike picked us up to go to the police station because E.W. filed charges against us for breaking his windshield, which we did not do. Daron just spat on it. Somebody yelled things at us at the store before we left. E.W. disappearing while we were being questioned at the police station. The phone call that the police had received about the accident. The accident ended up being my mother's, someone in a red suburban had run her off the road. The police officers left for the accident and let us go and said they would return to us later. I caught a ride home with Pastor Mike and Daron. Then Jaray came over in unc's car to get me because my mother was in the hospital. As we were leaving my house, someone smashed into us and hit me with a tire iron. They'd kidnapped me after knocking Jaray's head against the window breaking it which cut his face up. There was something over my head, a bag of some sort, pillowcase, maybe, they had my hands taped behind my back and a rope around my neck. Then the limb broke or they didn't have a good hold of the rope or something, and I fell down into the Saline river at Crain's Ferry. I'd managed to get out of the tape because the water helped loosen it up. I pulled the bag off my head and caught a branch to get out of the river. I noticed three white men on the other side. One jumped in after me so, I ran through the woods. They shot at me several times. I pulled the rope from my neck and managed to find my way to a road, which ended up being River Road, the road I live on. I ran down the road until I had realized that they may be close to me because of the way the road curved. I ran back into the woods and then the three men came driving by, slowly, in a green truck. They didn't see me, so they kept going. I then got back on the road and ran home, called the police and Officer Stanley came and picked me up and brought me to the hospital. At the hospital, I saw the same green truck I saw on River Road. Told Officer Stanley and he pursued the truck. I found out later that E.W. was the one driving the truck.

I told them everything that happened to me. They followed with other questions.

"Where is this Crain's Ferry?" Agent Benson asked.

"North on River Road, before the curve, there is a dirt road on the left, Ferry Road. Take it and it dead-ends at Crain's Ferry," unc said.

"Just before you get to Ferry Road, that land going north belongs to Mr. Evanson. He owns Evanson's Salt," Aunty Janie said.

"Okay, good to know," Agent Vitrees said.

"Now, ma'am, Mrs. Morre, what can you tell me about the accident, the red suburban?" Agent Benson asked.

"It's Ms. Morre, not Mrs. anyway, well, I was leaving work because, Janie," my mother pointed over to Aunty Janie. "Called me to tell me that Ralphie was being taken to the police station to be questioned about a broken windshield. So, I'd left work and as I was leaving, I noticed the red suburban. At first, I thought they were leaving as I was, but then they came up beside me honking like a mad person then hit my car, several times. Bumping my rear end and then sped up and hit the side of the car causing it to flip. I don't remember anything after that."

"Were you able to get a look at the driver?" Agent Benson asked.

"No."

"Was there anyone else in the Suburban?"

"I didn't see anyone."

"Okay. That's fine for now."

"Ralphie, tell me about your two friends, Daron and Jarod," Agent Benson said.

"I met Daron and Jarod at church. Not at the same time, but I had met Daron before going to church. He was playing basketball and I asked him if I could play. His dad, Pastor Mike asked if I would come to church. I agreed. So, that Sunday, Pastor Mike and Daron picked me up. When I went to church, that's when I met Jarod. Jarod Cache.

"And what is Daron's last name?" Agent Vitrees asked.

"You know, I don't recall him ever telling…"

Unc spoke up, "Musk. Pastor Mike's last name is Musk and Daron is his son. Daron Musk. Their family name used to me Musket, but a great grandfather of Mike's had it changed because people kept calling him Musketeer."

"Okay, thank you!" Agent Benson said.

Jaray walked into the living room and kneeled by unc.

"Jaray, right?" Agent Vitrees asked Jaray.

"Yeah."

"Tell me about the accident after picking up Ralphie."

"Well, when I backed out of Aunty Barb's driveway, I didn't see anybody. Then someone hit us. It just startled us at first. Then I saw someone come up and hit Ralphie with a tire iron. They pulled him out of the car and someone else jumped into the passenger side and knocked my head into the window. It broke the glass and cut up my face." He pointed to his face at the obvious bandage. "I have seventeen stitches, nothing major. They should take them out this week. I don't remember what happened after that. Aunty Janie said someone, a paramedic, going to work in Dallas, pulled up and took me to the hospital." Aunty Janie nodded her head in agreement.

"I almost forgot. We found a Klan newspaper in our yard!" I said.

"The Klansman?" Agent Benson asked.

"Yes, exactly!"

"Okay, that is probably connected. Do you still have the paper?"

"Yes, it's at my house."

"Okay, we will need to take a look at that."

"We'll get it to you," My mother said.

"Well, sounds like you guys have been through a lot the past couple of weeks. I think we have what we need for the moment. If we have any more questions, we'll get back to you!" Agent Benson said, standing and Agent Vitrees following his lead. Unc also stood. All three of them walked to the front door and unc walked them out.

"Good job, Ralphie!" my mother said.

"Well, it's what I can remember."

Unc came back in, shut the door, and said, "I hope they figure out who is behind all this. It's ridiculous. I have never in my life seen such hate, and I've lived here my entire life."

"It has to be something more than just hate," my mother said. "It just has to be, this can't be all about Ralphie's skin color."

"Yeah, I agree. There are other black folks who live here. Not many but there are some and they are much darker than Ralphie. They just don't get out around town too much," Aunty Janie said. "It may not be just about race."

"We should have told the agents that!" I said, thinking they would need that information to help with their investigation.

"I'll call them and tell them," unc said.

"Tell them about Ed Stetson and how he acted at the hospital," my mother said, suddenly remembering Ed.

"Okay, I will. He did act a little strange there didn't he after you mentioned the red suburban."

"Yes, he did."

"Could we go home now?" I asked my mother.

"Let me get cleaned up here, so Aunty Janie can help me," my mother said.

"Jaray better not have used all the hot water!" Aunty Janie said, sarcastically.

"I didn't!"

"Coming out here with just a towel covering your junk," Aunty said, laughing.

"I just wanted to let you know I was done, that's all. I didn't know those agents were here."

Aunty Janie wheeled my mother into the bathroom. She grabbed some towels and shut the door. We heard the shower turn on. Unc looked at us and then turned the television back on. The announcer is still talking about baseball. Jaray went to his room, I followed him. He turned on his stereo and I heard Tupac through the speakers. Not too loud this time because unc and Aunty Janie were home.

"What do you think they will find out?" I asked Jaray.

"I don't know, Ralphie, it's hard to tell right now. Aunty is right though. If there are other black folks here and they are not being targeted, it may not be about race."

"It's simply weird that they are trying to kill me. I did nothing to them."

"I know. With the FBI here investigating maybe they'll get to the bottom of it quickly and things can go back to normal."

"I don't think normal will ever happen. A new normal maybe. I was being lynched by white people for God's sake!"

"Sorry, you went through that. At least you came out alive."

"Yeah. I got lucky! It could have been worse."

"That's right, you could have been dead!"

Unc came in the room, "I couldn't get the agents on the phone, but I told Officer Madison to let them know. Anyway, I was going to run to the store, do you boys want anything? A soda?"

"Sure, unc, I'll take a soda. Out of the fountain, please," I said, thinking about a sweet snack too, but thought against it.

"Me too!"

"Me too? You're coming with me!" unc said to Jaray.

"Okay, then!"

"We'll be right back, Ralphie. Then when your Aunty and Mother are done, I'll give you guys a ride home. I told Office Madison that you guys are going home, and he is going to send an officer to watch your house."

"Good. Can't have the racist pricks, whatever they call themselves bother us anymore."

"Well, with all this police force watching everyone, I doubt anyone is going to bother you, or any of us for that matter," unc said. "Let's go Jaray!"

They walked out the door. I sat there on Jaray's lounge couch and listened to Tupac rapping lightly coming out of the speakers and thought about myself being against the world. I'd thought about life back in Harken. I didn't go through this much there and I lived there all my life. I would get into fights over some dumb clothes I wore but nothing like what happened a couple of weeks ago. I started bouncing my head to the music, some lady singing, me against the world! I thought to myself, it really is me against the world right now. I laid my head back on the couch and just listened to Tupac. My nerves still on edge, but the music seemed to be calming me.

"Ralphie, I've got your drink!" Jaray said, nudging me back awake, "You took a little nap while we were out working our bones off to get you a drink!"

"I didn't even realize I had fell sleep."

"Who does?" Jaray said, turning the stereo up a bit, Tupac rapping about his momma.

"Ran into your friend, Daron, at the store. Told him you'd be home later, and he said he was going to come by."

"Cool."

"I told them a brief version of what happened. He already knew most of it because of his dad."

Jaray started rapping with Tupac, "Even as a crack fiend, momma, you always was a black queen, momma!" He knew his mother loved him, but she was so unstable most of the time. She would come around and be sober and say she is changing for the better, but she'd end up drunk again.

"Ralphie, your mother is ready, are you?" Aunty Janie asked, standing in the doorway.

"Yes," I said as I grabbed my soda from the side table and jumped up. "See you later, Jaray!"

"Duces!" Jaray said, throwing up the peace sign as I walked out of the bedroom.

Unc was already pushing my mother's wheelchair out the front door. I walked up and joined them. When we got to the car, I helped unc get my mother in the passenger seat. He then folded up the wheelchair and placed it in the trunk. I jumped in the seat behind her. Unc got in the driver's seat and started the car. Put the gear in reverse and backed out of the driveway. Then he put the gear into drive. The officer waved as we drove by. No one waved back.

"Are you sure you guys are going to be okay by yourselves?" unc asked my mother, the conversation obviously continuing from another time before.

"Yes, Ronnie. I told you everything will be fine. They said there would be an officer outside the house, so we should be fine!"

"Okay, I just worry."

"Well, you're my older brother, not my father!"

"I'm not trying to be dad, Barb. I... I just don't want anything to happen to you two!"

"Don't worry, Ronnie. We'll be fine. Our family is full of fighters. You know that!"

"Yes, that we are!"

We arrived at my house and we saw the police car parked out front. Officer Madison didn't play around, he did everything he said he would. Unc pulled into the driveway and put the car into park. Paused for a moment, unclicked his seatbelt, paused again. Then said, "Barb, you don't think this has anything to do with..." he paused again. "What happened to you?"

"Of course not, Ronnie! We swore we would never bring that up!"

"Well, it's just strange that E.W. is saying that someone from the salt company hired them."

"I agree it's strange. But Ronnie, no one knows about that, except us."

"Ed Stetson knew about it, maybe he'd told someone!"

"I'm done talking about it, Ronnie!"

"Fine!"

Unc opened the door and got out of the car. He walked around to the back of the car, pulled the wheelchair from the trunk, and unfolded it. Then wheeled it to the passenger side door which he opened as my mother unclicked her seatbelt. I opened my door and got out to assist unc with getting my mother out of the car. I heard her whisper to unc that she was sorry.

"Okay, Barb. I'm sorry too, for bringing it up in front of Ralphie!"

There was something they knew that they didn't want anyone else to know. Since unc was bringing it up with me in earshot, it probably wasn't about me. Someone must have done something or maybe she knew something about Ed Stetson. Something that needed to be kept quiet. A family secret only shared between them.

"Ralphie, hold the wheelchair, will you?" unc said, picking up my mother.

"I've got it, unc. Waiting on you!"

"Oh!"

He placed my mother in the wheelchair and she thanked him. I started pushing her to the front door and unc followed us. Once at the front door, we noticed the door cracked open. Unc immediately stopped us. Whistled for the officer.

"Is everything okay?" the officer asked without getting out of the car.

"Looks like someone may have broken in!" unc replied.

The officer then radioed in about a possible break-in at our address. He stepped out of the car and walked up to the front door. Examining the door frame, he said, "Don't look like they broke anything here," pointing to the door frame around the latch.

"Yeah, maybe not but the door was cracked open when we got here!" my mother said.

"Let me go inside and check things out!" The officer said walking in the door, "Grayson Police department! Announce yourselves!" he said, holding his pistol holster open with his hand on his gun. Inside, he repeated himself.

"Don't shoot!" a familiar voice said.

"Put your hands up!" the officer shouted.

"Please don't shoot, I didn't do anything!"

"What are you doing here?"

"I came to see Ralphie!"

"What's your name?"

"I'm Daron Musk."

"Daron, what are you doing inside their house when they are not here?"

I heard Daron say his name, I knew I recognized the voice. I went into the house and saw the officer with his gun drawn and it pointed at Daron.

"It's okay officer, he is my friend," I said, walking toward Daron and the officer.

"Daron, what's going on?" I asked, curious as to why he was in the house.

"I came over and knocked on the door, the door was open a bit, and when I knocked it opened all the way. So, I came in and hollered your name and before I knew it, someone hit me on the head."

"Looks like they used that lamp," the officer said, pointing to the broken lamp on the floor. "Do I need to call a paramedic?"

"No, I'm okay, everything went black and the next thing I know, I am waking up to you saying to announce myself."

The officer said some inaudible things into his radio then looked at the lamp, "You boys need to step out so that I can clear the house."

"Okay," I said, Daron and I walk out of the front door to where my mother and unc were.

As the officer was clearing the house, another police car pulled up and then a black sedan behind them. I recognized Officer Madison right away. The windows on the sedan were too dark to see anyone. When they opened the door and got out, I realized that it was the two agents, Benson and Vitrees.

"Where's Officer Adams?" Officer Madison asked.

"He is inside, clearing the house," I said, noticing that Officer Madison didn't have a radio like the other officer.

Officer Madison went on into the house and joined Officer Adams. The agents stopped and started asking questions about who was in the house and why Daron was there. They then asked Daron about the E.W. situation from that Sunday at the Salt Palace. Daron confirmed my story.

"All clear!" Officer Adams said, coming out of the house followed by Officer Madison.

Agent Benson turned and looked at unc, "Mr. Morre, isn't the Crain's Ferry you guys were talking about north of here?"

"Yes. Just right up the road there," unc said, pointing to the north down River Road.

"We'd like to go down there and check it out, would you and Ralphie mind riding with us?" Agent Benson asked.

"Sure, but only if an officer is here with Barb."

"I'll stay, someone needs to be here in case someone comes back. I'll have another officer come and pick up my car and I'll stay inside, that is, if it's okay with Mrs. Morre." Officer Madison said.

"Ms. and that'll be just fine, if I can reach the coffee, I'll make us some," my mother said politely.

"Not to worry, ma'am, I'll help with that!"

"Okay, then, let's head down there, Mr. Morre and Ralphie, you can ride with us!" Agent Benson said.

"Is it alright if Daron comes along?" I asked Agent Benson.

"Sure."

# CHAPTER 9

# CRIME SCENE

U nc, Daron, and I got into the passenger side of the black sedan's back door. I slid over to the driver's side door and Daron slid in beside me, unc beside him. When he shut the door, Agent Benson asked, "Are we ready?"

"As ready as we'll ever be!" unc said.

Agent Benson started driving north on River Road. As we came up to Ferry Road, unc said to make a left. Agent Benson did as unc said. He had to slow the car down to about five miles an hour because the road was extremely bumpy. What used to be mud puddles are now dried-up big potholes. Slowing down some more, we could see the Saline River. It was the same location where they'd hung me to die.

"This is the spot where they were trying to kill me," I said, then I started pointing to the limb in front of the car that had broken from the tree. "I think that is the limb they had the rope around."

"Sure looks that way to me!" Agent Benson said, putting the car into park after he came to a complete stop in front of the tree. We all got out of the car and walked over to the tree limb. We could see where the rope had rubbed away some of the bark. The agents took some pictures and asked us not to touch anything. I looked downstream a bit to see if I could spot the location where I got out of the river, and I spotted it immediately.

"That's where I got out of the river!" I said, pointing to a limb hanging slightly in the river on the other side.

"Is there a way across the river?" Agent Vitrees asked.

"Yes, we'll have to go back to River Road and go north again," unc said.

"Okay, I think we've seen all we can see here!" Agent Vitrees said, putting away a camera.

We piled back into the car again, same seating. Agent Benson backed us out of Ferry Road. He started going north on River Road and noticed the road started curving to the east. It kept curving until we were going south.

"This takes us back to the river!" Agent Vitrees noticed.

"Yes, it does," I said.

"So, when you exited the river on this side, you ran into this road and ended up going back south toward your house?" Agent Vitrees questioned.

"Yes. I noticed the bridge and thought that I was coming close to the guys who had tried to kill me and then I dipped back into the woods. They came out and were driving slowly, looking on both sides but they didn't see me. Then they just took off. That's when I ran to my house and called the police."

"Is this city property?" Agent Benson asked.

"No, it belongs to Mr. Evanson. The man who owns Evanson Salt," unc answered. "He bought it at an auction when I was a kid. It used to belong to some KKK members. Klansman lived north of the river. Their kids would take Crain's Ferry to the other side to go to school back in the 1930s, way before the bridge was built."

Everyone listened to unc tell the story about Crain's Ferry.

"One day, Mr. Crain was taking the kids across the river for school and then shot holes in the floor of the ferry. All the Klansman kids and Mr. Crain drowned in the river."

"Why did he do that?" Agent Benson asked.

"Because the KKK killed Mr. Crain's son. Turns out Mr. Crain's son was dating a black woman and the Klan members found out and killed his son and the woman. Mr. Crain found them both hanging deep in the woods one day and decided he'd drown all their kids. The kids are buried in Erwin Cemetery. You can still see the graves today, but some of them are hard to read," unc finished.

"That's some story, is it true?" Agent Vitrees asked.

"The locals seem to think so and the graves seem pretty real to me!"

"Ralphie, take us through the woods and show us where you ran from," Agent Benson said to me, as he looked deep into the woods.

"Okay, it was right there, I think, where I came out of," I said, pointing to an opening. "The rope that they had used to hang me should be right down there somewhere."

We all started walking into the woods, everyone following my lead, Agent Benson behind me, close enough to step in front of me if he needed to. We walked probably one hundred yards before we found the rope. Agent Vitrees snapped a picture and picked up the rope and stuck it in a bag. I don't know where he had the bag, but one appeared. We walked another hundred yards or so and we could hear the river flow.

"We are getting close to the river," Agent Benson said.

"Yeah, over there you can see where they shot at me and it hit the tree. They shot, I think, three times and missed each time," I said, pointing at a tree trunk with a chunk of it missing. It looked like a bear or a big cat slapped it with its paws. Agent Vitrees took a few pictures with his camera and took some of the ground as well. We came up to the river and could see where we were on the other side moments ago.

"Luckily, you can swim, Ralphie. That river is moving fast!" Agent Vitrees said.

"Yeah, my mom used to take me down to Galveston a lot on the weekends so that I could swim in the ocean."

"I think we've seen all we can see here, don't you think?" Agent Benson said, turning around heading toward the car. We all followed his lead.

"I'll drop you guys off and go check in with Officer Madison. They picked up a couple more boys that are believed to be involved in your hanging, Ralphie, and I want to speak to them," Agent Benson said.

"He didn't mention that back at the house!" unc said. "Well, I guess with them clearing the house and all, he hadn't thought about it."

"Do you know who they are?" I asked.

"I'm not sure, I only just heard about it before we came to your house."

I begin thinking about those guys when we were on our way back to my house. I can only imagine the stories they would tell. They might even blame me for my own hanging, who knows?

We pulled up to my house, next to unc's car. We all got out of the car and went into the house. Officer Madison was sitting at the kitchen table with my mother, they were both sipping on coffee and talking.

"Officer Madison, could I speak with you outside please?" Agent Benson asked.

"Sure," he said, then turned to my mother. "I'll be right back."

"Take all the time you need."

"Mom, the agents said that the officers caught the other two guys who tried to kill me. "

"Yes, Officer Madison told me about it. They were waiting for the agents to come and question them."

"Do you know who they are?" unc asked my mother.

"Yes. E.W. Johns, Scout, and Troy Johnson. Officer Madison didn't want to talk with them before the FBI did. So, we'll learn more about it later. Officer Madison is going to stay here tonight and have someone here until everything is cleared up."

Officer Madison came back in, "The FBI are going to talk with those three men we arrested, and he said he will keep me informed through one of my officers."

"Good, I really want to know what this is all about."

"Me too," I said. "Let me know if you hear anything, I'm going to my room. I need some rest! I'll see you later unc, Daron, you're welcome to stay if you want."

"Nah, I'll catch a ride with your uncle if he's okay with that."

"That'll be fine, I need to talk with your dad anyway," unc said. I went on into my room.

After I shut the door to my room, I stood there a moment. I took a few deep breaths, trying to calm my nerves. I looked at my bed, then laid down, shoes and all. It wasn't long before I was fast asleep. I woke a couple of times, looking around my room, and went back to sleep. I dreamed I was falling and never reached the bottom. When I thought I was getting close to smashing into the ground, the ground would move out of the way and I would continue to fall.

"Don't move! Drop your weapon!" Officer Madison said, startling me awake. He flipped the light switch on, and I could see him and another man standing in my room. The man lowered his weapon to the floor and put his hands up behind his head.

"Let me guess, Farren Davis?" Officer Madison asked while taking the man's hands and putting them in handcuffs.

"Yes. The Johnsons talked, didn't they?" Farren asked.

"You know those boys, they are a bunch of rednecks, some KKK loving, drunks."

"Why did you hire them?"

"Lawyer!"

"So be it!" Officer Madison said, taking Farren out of my room, through the living room, and outside into the front yard, where a police car was just pulling into the driveway. Turns out, Officer Madison spotted Farren coming into the house and called it in. He then followed Farren around the house and into my room, where Farren was about to shoot me, but Officer Madison stopped him.

I went into my mother's room and she was still asleep, "Mom!"

"Ralphie, is everything okay?"

"Yes, someone by the name of Farren was just in my room…"

"Farren?" she said, puzzled. "Where's Officer Madison?"

"He caught the guy. The guy had his gun out and was about to shoot me when Officer Madison stopped him."

"Oh my God, are you okay?"

"Yes, mom I'm fine."

"Please help me into the wheelchair, Ralphie."

I helped my mother into the wheelchair and we both went into the living room. The agents had already made their way here. The officers and the agents were out in the front yard, talking. When they saw my mother and me at the front door, they made their way inside.

"Mrs. Morre. Farren Davis is the man we arrested in your house. He allegedly hired E.W. Johns, Scout, and Troy Johnsons to kill your son. He is currently being taken down to the station. He asked for a lawyer so we can't question him just yet," Agent Benson said. "We do believe that he is the reason for all of this."

"Even if, I am still going to keep an officer to cover you guys until we close this case," Officer Madison said. "Okay?"

"Thank you! Not only for that but for saving my son. If you weren't here, he would have killed him. I still don't understand why they want to kill Ralphie. I see Farren all the time at work, he has even asked me out a few times and I've turned him down. He is one of the board members for the salt company. You don't think he is mad at me because of me turning him down, do you?" my mother asked.

"I'm not sure, I guess it is possible!" Officer Madison said.

"Yes, and it turns out that he owns a red suburban," Officer Adams added.

"He's the one who ran me off the road?"

"Yes, it seems that way," Agent Benson said.

"Officer Adams get Farren down to the police station and get him his phone call. I want to talk to him as soon as possible, so he'll need his lawyer fast," Officer Madison said, and the agents agreed.

Officer Adams walked out to his car and got in. He pulled out of the driveway and headed toward the police station. The night was dark except for the red and blue lights flashing in the agent's car.

\*\*\*

After everyone left and it was just my mother, Officer Madison, and me, I went into the kitchen and made some hot dogs. Boiled the franks on the stove and heated up a can of chili. Grabbed some loaf bread because we didn't have any hot dog buns. I pulled three plates from the cabinet and put three loaf slices on each plate. Placed a frank in the center of each slice and poured a spoonful of chili on each one. I grabbed some shredded cheese and sprinkled some on the chili, the chili still hot, melting the cheese before I brought the plates to the kitchen table. Mom said grace and we all thanked God and ate our chili dogs.

"Ralphie, you make a mean chili dog," Officer Madison said, cramming his mouth full.

"Crap, I forgot about our drinks," I said, getting up from my seat going to the cabinet to get three glasses. I pulled the tea from the refrigerator and filled each glass then carried mom and Officer Madison's to the table and went back for mine. Officer Madison got a big drink, mom just sipped hers. I was about to sit down at the table when we heard a knock on the front door.

"I'll see who it is," Officer Madison said, setting down his tea glass. He got up and headed to the front door and reached for his gun.

"Hello, Barb?" a voice from the door said.

"It's unc," I said.

Officer Madison removed his hand from his gun, unlocked the door, and opened it. Unc came rushing in.

"Are you guys okay? I just heard what happened."

"We're fine, Ronnie."

"They caught a guy in my room, unc. Trying to kill me, he had a gun and everything."

"This is crazy. Why are they doing this?" unc asked.

"We are trying to figure that one out," Officer Madison said.

"Well, I'm glad you're all okay."

"God has got his arms around us, Ronnie, and you won't believe who it was."

"Yes, he does," Officer Madison added, talking about God's hands.

"Who was it?" unc asked, sitting down at the kitchen table.

"Farren Davis," mom said. "It probably does have something to do with me turning him down."

Unc shifted in his seat at the table. I grabbed another glass and filled it with tea and brought it to him. He gladly accepted and said, "I knew it."

We sat around the table and talked about chili dogs, God, and the things that have been happening. Mainly the things that have been happening to me.

Ring!

Ring!

"Hello!" I said into the phone.

"This is Officer Adams for Officer Madison."

"It's for you," I said, handing the phone to Officer Madison.

"Officer Madison here."

"Okay, send an officer here and I'll come up. Okay, bye!"

Hanging up the phone, Officer Madison said. "Farren Davis's lawyer is at the station and the agents are about to go in and talk with them. A uniformed officer is coming to relieve me so that I can be there too, when they question Farren."

"So, he lawyered up right after you arrested him?" unc asked Officer Madison.

"Yes, as soon as I asked why he hired them."

Unc was shaking his head in disbelief. My mother just sat there in her wheelchair, also in disbelief.

"I have to get some air," I said scooting my chair out from the kitchen table. I stood and walked to the front door.

"Ralphie," my mother said. I stopped but didn't look back. "Everything's going to be alright. I know we've been through a lot since we moved here. Hang in there because it gets the darkest before the dawn."

I started walking again, "I know mom." I opened the front door and stepped out onto the porch. The warm breeze hit me, and I felt a sudden urge to run, but I didn't. I just stood there, staring into the starry sky. I thought about the ocean in Galveston and how good it would feel to be in it right now, without a care in the world. I thought about the girl I met on the beach one summer. Brandy. She was from Oklahoma. A Native American. A member of the Choctaw tribe. Her family was vacationing there on the beach for a week. We hung out all night and watched the stars and she, too, said that it gets the darkest before the dawn.

Yes, it does, I said silently talking to myself as if Brandy could hear me.

"Yes, what does?" unc said walking out while overhearing me.

"The darkness. It gets the darkest before the dawn. Looking up and down River Road. It's dark out!"

"Yeah."

"I'm heading home, do you want me to send Jaray over for a little while, so you can have some company?"

"Only if he wants to come over."

"Okay, I'll see you later."

"On second thought, don't worry about it. I think I'm just going to go back to bed."

"Okay. We'll just come over tomorrow. See you later."

"See ya, unc"

A police car pulled up out front. I walked back inside. My mother and Officer Madison are still sitting at the table.

"The other officer is here!" I said to Officer Madison.

"Okay, thanks," he said, excusing himself. He went outside and sent the other officer to the porch. My mother told me to invite him in.

"I'm Officer Glaves. Thanks for inviting me in. Sorry, you guys are going through all this. Officer Madison said he'll return after they talk to the suspect."

"Not a problem. You're welcome anytime," my mother said.

"I'm going to go lay down mom. Are you going to be okay?"

"Yes, Ralphie, I'll be fine. If I need anything, I'm sure this kind officer, Glaves, is it?" he shook his head. "Will help me with it. You get some sleep. You need your rest."

I walked into my room and saw my bed. It looked so relaxing. I picked up a notebook and pen and laid down on my back. I lay there for the longest before I thought of anything to write. I wanted to write songs or poems, but then I figured the most important thing right now was to write my story. To tell my story about what happened here on River Road. I started writing. Starting from the beginning, right after I'd moved from Harken to Grayson. To River Road. A house owned by the Evanson's Salt Company. My mother took a secretary job at the salt company. She said it paid twice as much as the job in Harken. So here we are. Being terrorized by Nazi loving rednecks. I eventually drifted off to sleep. I dreamed I was falling again, but this time I actually hit the ground, running. I had the rope around my neck again and people were chasing me, wearing business suits and KKK hoods. Just before I woke up, Jaray was wearing a crown like the one Notorious B.I.G. wore during his last photoshoot before he was killed back in March. I asked Jaray why he was wearing the crown, but he just kept saying, Ralphie, wake up.

"Ralphie, wake up," Jaray said, continuing to shake me.

"I'm up, dang!"

"Guess who is here and is not drunk?"

"That could only be one person if it's family."

"You guessed it, my momma fool, she rode over here with unc and me!"

"Man, I had a dream you were wearing a crown like the one Biggie wore."

"I love it when you call me big papa!" Jaray said, trying to mimic Notorious B.I.G.!

# CHAPTER 10

# AN UNEXPECTED VISITOR

When Jaray and I went into the living room, Aunty Charlene, unc, and Aunty Janie, and my mom were talking about what has been going on. Aunty Charlene hasn't been around, so they were informing her on what had happened. The last few times I remember seeing her, she was drunk. But right now, sitting on the couch, talking with her siblings, she seemed okay. Happy. Normal, even. You could tell Jaray was happy to see her. He was sitting so close to her and they were hugging each other. Almost like a normal family would. I pray she stays sober.

I slept most of the night and I feel fully rested now, even though less than twenty-four hours ago someone was in my room with a pistol about to kill me. I don't even know the reasons as to why they are so eager to kill me. What have I done to have them come after me? I hadn't done anything that I know of. If they have a problem with my skin color, then the problem is with them, not me. Aunty Charlene has the same skin complexion as me. I never heard of her having any issues like I'm having here. And she has lived here all her life. She wasn't born here like my mother. Aunty Charlene was born in California somewhere in San Diego County. My grandfather had an affair with a black woman named, Wanita, while he was in the military. Wanita ended up pregnant with Charlene. After Charlene was born, Wanita passed away. Papa brought Aunty Charlene home and my grandmother raised her like her own. Never acted differently toward her, not even once. Charlene is the oldest, then unc, Aunty Mary, and then my mother. Unc has two kids, both grown now and living somewhere close to Dallas. Aunty Charlene just has Jaray. Aunty Mary has three kids with my dad's brother, my double first cousins, and my mother just has me.

The phone started ringing and unc got up and answered it, "Hello," he said into the receiver.

I wondered what was being said on the other end of the phone. Unc just stood there listening to whoever it was. My mother looked at him waiting on him to say something. Aunty Janie couldn't help herself, "Well, who is it, Ron?"

"Hold on a sec," unc said. "No, not you, my nosy wife!"

Aunty Janie sat back on the couch and crossed her arms. Aunty Charlene was closer to unc and I could see that she was trying to listen to what the caller was saying. I couldn't tell by her facial expression if she was getting any information or not. My mother still looking at unc, impatiently waiting for him to tell her who was on the phone and what they were talking about. Jaray still sitting by his mother, where he hasn't moved an inch since we came into the living room. I was standing by my mother before unc got up to answer the phone, then I took his seat. Looking at him I couldn't tell if he was hearing good news or what.

By the time he had hung up the phone, everyone was catching their breath. It seemed like we all held our breath while he was talking or listening to whoever it was on the phone. Everyone looked at unc and he walked over to me, signaling a *get out of my chair* motion with his hand, like an umpire saying I was out. I got up and walked toward the kitchen. I wanted to get a drink; I knew I could hear him if he started talking. I reached into the cabinet and pulled out a glass. Opened the refrigerator and saw that there wasn't any tea. There were cans of coke, though. I pulled a can out and opened it. As I was pouring it into my glass, I heard unc start talking. I could only imagine everyone still holding their breath and waiting on him to say something.

"Well…" he started. "I don't know how to even say this. That was Officer Madison on the phone." I walked back into the living room sipping my coke. Aunt Charlene was acknowledging what unc has just said. Which confirmed she could hear who was on the phone.

"The Johnson brothers just let it all out. Their stories collaborate with each other's. Farren Davis hired them and E.W. to act like they were the KKK to go after a black kid that lives with a white woman. Which seemed to be Ralphie. They were never told any names, though, because Farren didn't know their names. They assumed it was you and Ralphie. They noticed Ralphie when he was walking around, and they followed him to see where he lived. Scout then sat down the road to see if there was a white woman living here, too." Unc looked at my mother, "When you came home, Barb, they saw that you were white and automatically assumed you and Ralphie were who Farren was talking about." He paused a moment and took some light breaths and continued. "The Johnson brothers then threw a Klan newspaper into the yard here. Hoping to stir up something, to see what would happen. When they realized nothing happened, they had to figure out what else to do. Then when Ralphie walked into the Salt Palace on that Sunday, E.W. saw an opportunity to escalate matters then. He called Ralphie a nigger and his friends nigger lovers."

"That's the names he called us. Daron and Jarod wouldn't tell me what E.W. said to them inside the Salt Palace before they came out, I figured that's what he said," I interrupted.

"Anyway, E.W. told the Johnsons about them spitting on his windshield, so they decided to break the windshield and say that Ralphie and his nigger loving friends did it," unc swallowed hard. He never liked the n-word.

"E.W. went to the police station and filed a report against them. The boys were out walking, and Officer Madison went to find Pastor Mike because he was told Daron was one of the kids that broke the windshield. Pastor Mike left to help with looking for them and spotted them at the convenience store."

"Yeah, and someone said don't let the sun set on your black ass," I added. "Just before we left the store."

"That was E.W. and the Johnson brothers, they're the ones that yelled that and they were in a green truck," unc said. "Officer Madison recognized them. That's why they found them so quickly. Not because Officer Stanley pursued the green truck from the hospital. It was because Officer Madison knew who was in the truck. So, when Officer Stanley radioed the pursuit in, Officer Madison just went to E.W.'s house and waited for him to get home."

I imagined the look on E.W.'s face when he reached his house and found Officer Madison sitting there waiting for him. Some criminals are just unlucky. Take Farren for instance, he was here with a gun ready to kill a kid, but unbeknown to him, Officer Madison was here too, waiting.

"After questioning E.W., they were able to pick up the Johnsons, but they were hiding on their father's farm out on twenty-seven in a red barn. They eventually found them and brought them in, put them both in separate interrogation rooms. They both told the same story as E.W. giving Farren

Davis's name as the person who hired them," unc paused. I didn't know if it was for dramatic effect or because that was everything that Officer Madison said. Everyone was on the edge of their seat.

"Farren hasn't talked to anyone except for his lawyer all night. They are waiting for his lawyer to give them the okay but, he hasn't yet. Officer Madison said he'd call as soon as he hears something. I figured after Barb turned him down when he asked her for a date a few times, that he got mad and started coming after them. You said he got really upset and Ed had to calm him down and leave you alone. Anyway, officer Madison said he was going to send someone to relieve Officer Glaves. Where is he by the way?"

"He is in the guest room. I told him we were okay and that he could sleep in there, he's been asleep a while now," my mother answered. "He is such a sweet kid."

"Officer Glaves, huh, I think I know his father," unc said.

I started thinking about what my mother and unc were talking about in the car. It must have been about Farren asking her out and she didn't want me to know. He must have been a little too pushy and Ed had to do something to put a stop to it. I don't know, and I probably will never know, she doesn't like to share that stuff with me, because I get upset and want to hurt them for treating my mother that way.

Jaray finally got up and went into the kitchen, he, too got himself something to drink. He also made his mother a glass of water. She had asked him if he would get her something to drink. Jaray didn't want to get her anything strong. Anything that would make her think of alcohol. He just filled her glass full of water and brought it to her. She looked at it, took it from him, and began drinking it. Before he sat down next to her again, she had already finished drinking the entire glass of water. She sat the glass down on the coffee table, hard. She looks like she was sweating, and it wasn't even hot in the house. I guess you get that way when all you drink is alcohol.

"Are you okay, Charlene?" Aunty Janie asked?

"Yes. I'm fine. Just having an episode, it'll pass."

"Do you need your shot?" unc asked.

"No, it'll pass!"

"Shot! What shot?" Jaray asked, a little too excitedly.

"Don't worry, Jaray, it's nothing. I'll be okay."

"It's never nothing, mom. There is always something. Please don't tell me not to worry. I do worry about you, you're my mother!"

"Well, I have it under control, so there is no need to worry, son."

"Fine."

Unc got up and went over to Aunty Charlene and leaned down by her. He whispered something to her, I couldn't make it out. They both raised up and she grabbed her purse.

"Where are you going?" Jaray asked.

"We'll be right back, Jaray, just relax," unc said following Aunty Charlene out the front door.

"What the hell is going on with those two! They never tell me anything when it comes to my mother!"

"Jaray, it's okay. Your mother is doing the best she can. She is going to be staying with us for a while and we are going to help her get better. She was diagnosed with diabetes about a month ago and has been battling it and drinking. A bad combo," Aunty Janie said, moving closer to Jaray and putting her arm around him. "Everything is going to be okay."

"God works in mysterious ways," my mother added.

I see what my mother was talking about. Everyone prayed Aunty Charlene would quit drinking and now she has diabetes, which to manage properly, she'll have to quit drinking. Some things are more important than others. She chose to drink over her kid but now, she'll have to choose not to drink in order to manage her diabetes correctly, or she could possibly die. I'm pretty sure she doesn't want that.

"Yes, he does," Aunty Janie said. "He does work mysteriously."

The phone rang again, and Aunty Janie jumped up to answer it. Officer Glaves walked into the living room. Unc and Aunty Charlene were out in Aunty Janie's car. My mother and I looked at Aunty Janie as she said hello to the caller.

"He's unavailable at the moment, is there an update?" she paused for a moment so the caller could speak. We all assumed it was Officer Madison. "Yes, yes, I understand," she said as she hung up the phone.

"Well, what is it, Janie?" my mother asked.

"That was Officer Madison, Farren is not going to talk to them."

"Now we'll never know the truth as to why they were trying to kill us," my mother said, her voice revealing the anger within her for not having an answer. We've been through a lot in the last couple of weeks. Now it seemed we weren't going to get an answer as to why we've been through what we've been through. With Farren not talking many questions are going to go unanswered.

The phone rang again. Aunty Janie raced to pick it up, "Hello!"

Unc and Aunty Charlene came walking in the front door. Aunty Charlene looked a lot better. Unc walked over to Aunty Janie, "Is that Officer Madison?"

Aunty Janie shook her head no. Everyone looked puzzled. The only person that has been calling is Officer Madison.

"Okay..." Aunty Janie listened some more. "That would be wonderful."

Someone then knocked on the door. Unc walked over and opened the door and standing there was Officer Stanley, "I'm here to relieve Officer Glaves."

Officer Glaves walked out and greeting Officer Stanley. Officer Stanley and Officer Glaves stood outside a minute before parting ways and Officer Stanley came into the house.

"Pardon my intrusion," he said.

"No intrusion," my mother countered.

Aunty Janie had hung up the phone and started telling everyone who the caller was and why they had called. "That was Mary, she said she was coming up and she didn't care what anyone said."

Aunty Mary and unc had gotten into a big fight about a year ago. Aunty Mary thought Jaray should come and live with her, and unc thought that Jaray should be here close to his mother. The fight ended with the both of them not wanting to see each other anymore.

"She wants to come up and help in any way she can, and she wants to apologize to you Ron, only in person."

"Well, she needs to. She was in the wrong," unc said.

"With an attitude like that things are not going to get any better," Aunty Janie said.

"How'd she even know about what was going on here?" unc asked.

"I called her!" Jaray said, standing up.

"You called her? When?" unc questioned.

"This morning, before we came over here. I was excited about my mother coming by and wanted to tell Aunty Mary. Get mad all you want; you guys need to stop acting like a bunch of kids. Blood is all we have and with everything that's been going on, you should put that meaningless stuff behind you."

"Jaray, you're such a wise kid, I'm proud of you." Aunty Charlene said, walking over to give him a hug.

"Mom, you need to stop all this nonsense you've been doing, drinking and whatnot before you lose everything. You didn't even tell me about the diabetes," Jaray continued. "Unc didn't even tell me and he has been there for me most of my life, and him taking me in the last year was the best thing for me. But right now, our family is in trouble and Aunty Mary and unc need to put aside their differences and come together so that we can save our family."

"I'm sorry, Jaray, you're right. When Mary comes up, I'll drop it all. She doesn't even have to apologize. It's selfish of me to even keep that going."

"I'm sorry you have to hear all this," my mother said to Officer Stanley.

"It's okay, ma'am, I was just thinking about how you guys remind me of my family. I guess every family has their drama, right?"

"Yeah, they do. You were just dropped right in the middle of it all. So just make yourself at home." My mother said with a welcoming smile.

"You guys make it too easy."

I went into my room and picked up my pen and notebook. While everyone in the living room was getting all emotional, I wanted to express my emotion in my notebook. I just really wanted to be alone. Sometimes a guy needs that, just alone time. I haven't had much alone time while running around trying to avoid death. I took this opportunity to sit alone in my room and write about the last couple of weeks.

Who knows, maybe I'll turn it into a book one day. My Tales on River Road and Racism, I would call it. By Ralph Parsons. I sat in my room for a good thirty minutes before Jaray came looking for me. I hadn't heard the phone ring. I barely heard him coming into my room.

"Hey, Ralphie, whatcha writing, war stories?"

For a short moment, I thought about the Tupac song, Tradin' War Stories. That would be a good name for my book, but then I thought against it. "No, just writing. What's up?"

"Well, Officer Madison called and wants us to meet him at the courthouse! Something about a lawyer and Evanson's Salt. They didn't elaborate much so, everyone is waiting, so come on."

"Okay."

I put my book down and joined Jaray, we walked out of my room and back into the living room where everyone was ready to go. My mother looked at me, sometimes I would think she was about to cry, and then she would look away. If there were any tears, she'd suck them back in. That's probably where I got my toughness, from my momma. She could be a nice little lamb one minute and a raging bull or better yet a lion, the next. I followed everyone out to the driveway. Unc helped my mother in the passenger seat of Aunty Janie's car and put my mother's wheelchair in the trunk. I jumped in the back seat behind my mother and Aunty Janie got in on the other side. Unc hopped in the driver's seat. Aunty Charlene and Jaray got in her car. Officer Stanley stood on the porch and radioed something in. Probably that he was stranded at the house and everyone was leaving, I don't know. Unc then rolled down the window, "Do you want to ride with us?" he asked Officer Stanley.

"No, thanks, I have a car coming."

"Okay."

Unc pulled out of the driveway and we headed downtown. The courthouse is in the center of downtown and looks like a mini-Capitol building. Sometimes people refer to it as the Capitol. You could see the top of it from about a mile away, maybe more. It's the place where people learn their fate. We were on our way to learn ours.

"I'm curious what this is about. Why are they dragging us all down to the courthouse?" unc asked. "They could have just told us on the phone!"

"It must be much more important than that, Ron."

When we made it to the courthouse, everyone walked in together as I pushed my mother's wheelchair. Officer Madison met us at the door.

"There is some very important information that is coming from Mr. Evanson's personal attorney Dexter

Schwartz," Officer Madison said, escorting us to a conference room behind a courtroom.

# CHAPTER 11

# COURT HOUSE MEETING

W hen we were all in the conference room, we all sat around a huge table. Every chair, ten of them to be exact, matched and felt amazingly comfortable. The table looked like it was made of an oak tree, stained with Early American stain, it shined as the sunlight hit it. The window blinds on all four windows have been raised, allowing the sun to light the room. In the room was my family and Officer Madison talking about what this could all be about until a tall burly man came in the room, he carried a briefcase, black, matching his suit. Agent Benson walked in behind him, giving me the impression that the burly man was an FBI agent, too. They both sat at the head of the table, the burly man placed the briefcase in front of him and steadied his hands on the latches. The room went really quiet. Everyone looked at him.

Officer Madison excused himself, "I'll leave you guys to it."

"Hello, I'm Dexter Schwartz, I'm the personal attorney for Lee Evanson and his estate," he said. "Lee Evanson was the majority owner of the Evanson's Salt Company and also owns well-over one thousand acres of land around Grayson. I've asked for you guys to come down because I want to personally apologize for what members of Evanson's Salt Board have done to your family. I'm sorry."

"That doesn't fix anything," unc said. "Look at my sister in the wheelchair and my nephews with the bandages on as if it's their clothes."

"My baby, I can't believe they did that to you and look what they did to Ralphie. Those evil bastards," Aunty Charlene said, looking at both me and Jaray.

"I know that my apology does not fix anything," Mr. Schwartz said, pulling folders from his briefcase. "Nor will what I am going to share with you today. But I wanted to start there to let you know that the Evanson Salt Company, Mr. Evanson, had nothing to do with what happened to your family. Those board members acted on their own will and have since been removed from the board."

"Those board members," unc said. "You said those board members? Right? As in more than one?"

"Yes. There were actually three board members involved in this situation."

Agent Benson adjusted his chair and started speaking, "We arrested Edward Stetson early this morning, just before three am. He was caught trying to suffocate Mr. Evanson. A nurse walked in on him and she called security who detained Stetson as he was trying to leave until we arrived."

"Oh, my word!" my mother said, gasping. Shocked that Ed Stetson was involved. She has worked with him daily since we moved here. "What is Ed's involvement in this whole thing besides him trying to suffocate Mr. Evanson?"

"Between him and Mr. Davis, they both played equal parts in the organizing and hiring E.W. Johns, and the Johnson brothers to identify and murder your son, by only identifying him by his skin color," Agent Benson said. "The name has only been brought to our attention as of 8:30 this morning."

"I'm not following... the name? Ralphie's name has just only this morning," unc said pointing down at the desk, "Been brought to your attention?"

"Mr. Davis," Dexter Schwartz began elaborating, "A cousin to Mr. Evanson, broke into my office safe at my office building and made a copy of Mr. Evansons will about a month ago. We only learned of that from Edward Stetson. The will states that Mr. Evanson's estate is to be willed to his grandson upon his death. He did not leave a name, only that his grandson is of negro descent and is living with a white woman. He didn't want to put the name in this will because he didn't want people becoming greedy and try to harm his grandson. However, the will goes on to say that upon Mr. Evanson's death that if his grandson was unable to inherit his estate, due to the death of his grandson or some other reason, then the estate is to be managed by the Evanson's Salt Company Board of Directors for one year and then the estate is to be passed to Farren Davis, his cousin." Mr. Schwartz took a moment to clear his throat, "There is another will which is to be added to this one, and the additional will says that the safety deposit box number seventeen at Grayson Community Bank is to be willed to Dexter Schwartz. Now, me being Dexter Schwartz, and I knew of the will, and that Mr. Evanson passed, I opened the safety deposit box and found this folder," he picked up a folder that looked empty. "And in this folder is yet another will, also an addition, only it was prepared by a law office in Dallas on Mr. Evanson's behalf. It appears that he didn't even want me to know this information. In this additional will, it reveals the name of his grandson."

Everyone seemed to ease in just a little so that they would not miss hearing the name of Mr. Evanson's negro descent grandson. I remember thinking to myself, that whoever this grandson is, he is about to inherit a butt load of money and land.

Agent Benson interrupted, "However, the name cannot be revealed at this time, at least not until we apprehend the third board member, Samantha Rowlands. She does not have a big role but a role all the same. She's the person who drove the red suburban the day Barbara was run off the road."

"Sam. How could she? That's a pretty big role in my opinion!" my mother said.

"Yeah, I agree, that's a pretty big role!" agreed Aunty Janie.

"Sorry, I didn't mean it that way."

My mother just shrugged it off and said, "What was she getting out of it?"

"Mr. Davis offered her a percentage of his share once he received it. They all assumed that the grandson was your son, Ralphie. However, we know as of today and as do they, minus Samantha, at least until she is found, that Ralphie is not Mr. Evanson's grandson," Agent Benson said.

The room went quiet, everyone seemed to be deep in thought.

"I have agents and local police out searching for Samantha Rowlands as we speak. I figure they'll find her within an hour," Agent Benson added "Hopefully!"

"So, you brought us down here to tell us that Ralphie was being targeted, not because he is biracial but because he matches the description," unc said. "And now, you still have one more person to apprehend. How did you find out about her?"

"No, I brought you down here to clear up some things, I figured you would have wanted to know, and Ed Stetson told us that Mr. Davis has stolen the will and that if he could get rid of the grandson, then he would give Ed and Samantha a percentage of the estate once he received it. What they didn't realize was that the three men they hired would be as unorganized as they were. They publicly made a scene which ultimately led to their arrest. And they didn't account for how tough the Morre family is."

"You got that right!" Aunty Charlene said looking around the room.

Someone came into the room and whispered into Agent Benson's ear. He looked over at unc and paused, looked around at everyone else, then said, "There is a phone call I must take. Please excuse me." He got up from the table and walked out of the room. Mr. Schwartz just sat there reading quietly to himself.

My mother noticeably upset about all this said, "Ralphie, please take me outside I need to get some fresh air."

"I can open a window. You want me to open a window?" I said, looking over at the windows and pointing.

"Ralphie, please."

"Okay, sure mom," I said, rising up out of my chair walking over to her wheelchair, unlocking the wheels. I started pulling her back away from the table and then we headed toward the door while Jaray went and held it open for us.

"Thanks, Jaray!" my mother said as we rolled through the door.

After leaving the conference room, I could see Agent Benson on the phone in an office across the hall. He didn't seem upset or anything, he was just casually talking. It could have only been his wife if he's married, or maybe a longtime friend.

I pushed my mother's wheelchair into the courtyard and parked her by a bench, where I sat myself. We sat there in silence listening to the birds, the occasional car passing by. I thought about what Mr. Schwartz said and how the agents were still looking for someone named Samantha. Someone my mother knew as well. I mainly thought about the reasons they were doing all this. Their craving for money, power, and control.

My grandmother came to mind when I thought about money, 'The love of money is the root of all evil!' she used to say, and she was exactly right. Ed Stetson, Farren Davis, and Samantha Rowlands were after Mr. Evanson's money, his control of the Evanson's Salt Company. What would they have done with the control and the money? They would have done the same things they were doing now, fighting to keep the money and the control. It would be a never-ending battle for them as it is for those fighting racism and feminism. The list goes on just like river of water flowing, never-ending and always finds itself in a bigger and deeper area.

"Ralphie, you know I love you right?" my mother said between the birds tweeting.

"Yes, mom, you know that I know that!"

"I'm sorry I moved us here."

"Mom, we may have been in some terrible circumstances the last couple of weeks, but we can't let that hold us back from moving forward."

"Yeah, but it's nothing like we were dealing with in Harken. At least we had a little freedom there."

"No mom, it's nothing like Harken, you're right about that. But freedom is something we'll probably never find, anywhere. Not when the world must fight for the rights of everyone. Because, sooner or later, we'll all be fighting for the right to fight!"

"Ralphie, I don't know where you are going with all that. I'm just saying that ninety percent of our time here has been a nightmare."

"Yeah, I would say so too, but you're the one that was born here, not me."

"Oh, now you have jokes!"

"Barb!" unc yells out the door from the courthouse.

"Let's go, Ralphie, it's your uncle."

I wheel mom up to the door and unc said, "Agent Benson is back, and he has an update, I didn't want them to start without you in there! So."

"Thanks, Ronnie."

Back inside the conference room, everyone was seated. The room air cool to my heated skin, the shuffling of papers breaking the silence that filled the room.

"Turns out," Agent Benson said. "Samantha has been apprehended. She was spotted heading toward Dallas. Of all vehicles she could have been driving, she was driving Mr. Davis's red suburban. A state trooper clocked her driving twenty miles over the posted speed limit. After running her name and finding the APB we had on Samantha Rowlands, she was placed under arrest and is cooperating."

"Good, this means we can go home and relax," my mother said. "I'm so ready. I don't know if I could even go back to work at Evanson's Salt Company after all this."

"Yeah, I don't want you to. People over there seem to be too greedy," I said, agreeing with my mother.

Agent Benson turned and looked out the door and then said, "Well, since we have everyone in custody. I may even head back home. I'll stop on my way to have a conversation with Samantha Rowlands, but I can do all the paperwork from my own office in Dallas."

"Thank you for all your help, Agent Benson," my mother said.

Putting out his hand to shake Agent Benson's hand, unc said, "Yes, thank you!"

Everyone seated at the conference table stood as Aunty Janie started pushing my mother toward the door when Dexter Schwartz began speaking.

"Now, I still have a little tiny, but important piece of information to share with you."

The room again went still and quiet. The sun is still shining through the windows. People still walking in the hall, we could hear their footsteps over the silence in the room. Dexter pulled a folder out and opened it up, removing the single sheet of paper, he said, "Mr. Lee Evanson had one grandchild, a boy, fathered by his one and only son, Leroy Evanson."

"Leroy Evanson was a victim of an unsolved homicide about sixteen years ago, in Dallas, however, Mr. Lee Evanson wrote in his will that Leroy admitted to him about raping a black girl and getting her pregnant."

Aunty Charlene, although, she has a dark complexion, went pale white. My heart started racing, I looked a Jaray. He looked at his mother, at her paleness, and said, "Momma, are you alright?"

Mr. Schwartz continued, "The young man that Lee Evanson claims to be his grandson, is none other than, Jaray Morre."

The whole family said nothing, everyone was shocked. Silence again filled the room. My mother fell forward, Aunty Janie, rushed to her care. Unc walked over to Aunty Charlene, Jaray seemed confused. The words that he appeared to say, only reaching his lips, his right hand on his chest, as to say what his voice couldn't say, "Me?"

Aunty Charlene then stood, looking at Jaray, and said, "I don't want his evil money! Jaray, you're not taking it! This is just not going to happen!"

"Momma, this could be good for us! I'm sorry that happened and this doesn't make it right, but if I am Mr. Evanson's grandson then this is rightfully mine."

Mr. Schwartz stood and faced Jaray and Aunty Charlene, "As it stands right now, legally, whether you are or are not Mr. Lee Evanson's grandson, you are now the owner of his estate and I am legally your personal lawyer unless you say otherwise."

Jaray looks at his mother, and she looks back at him. They both have tears in their eyes and are flooded with emotion. My mother and Aunty Janie calm down, searching for words to say, but they too, cannot put into words what they are feeling. Unc, standing next to Aunty Charlene, rubbing her back, speaks, "This is unexpected. I think later today, we all need to get together and discuss some things," he paused. "Plus, I think we need to let Mary know, she should be here by now, probably looking for us."

"Mr. Schwartz, if you would excuse us," Aunty Janie said.

"Sure ma'am!" he said, gathering his files and folders while stuffing them into his briefcase. Closing and latching it, he said, "Jaray, I know you're underage and that's not going to stop me from doing what you asked of me, however, there are legal documents that will need to be signed by your legal guardians. They will need to be available to sign by Friday so could you and your guardians meet me here at nine o'clock on Friday morning?"

"Yes."

Dexter Schwartz then waved a quick wave at us and walked out of the conference room, briefcase in hand.

Aunty Charlene then spoke, only quietly, "I hate that man for what he has done to me. At times I thought it was my fault, that maybe I led him on. But I know I didn't deserve to be raped. I don't know why I would even think I led him on, I never met him before he grabbed me at that party. All his friends cheered him on. I was so drunk I don't know if I put up a fight or not. I just remember telling him no, no... he did not stop. His friends kept cheering him on. I hate him for that. God gave me you, Jaray. I don't know if I could ever forgive that man for what he has done to me, but I have you, and if you want to keep this money, then keep it."

"Thank you, momma. I'm sorry that it happened, too. I wish it hadn't even if I wouldn't be here. But maybe this money can get you the help you need and bring us back together. I love you!"

"I love you, too, Jaray. More than you'll ever know. I'm sorry I've been a bad mother..." Jaray cut her off, "You're not a bad mother, you're a mother in pain, and looking at me only reminds you of that pain. I can live with that, but I can't live without you!"

They both start hugging each other with much-needed affection and they let their tears flow. Unc already hugging them, my mother and Aunty Janie, now crying begin to move toward them as well. I couldn't help but join them. We all hugged as one big family.

The hugging and crying lasted for about another five minutes before someone came and knocked on the door. We all turned, wiping away the tears to see who was at the door. It was Officer Madison.

"Mr. Morre," he said, and both unc and Jaray said, simultaneously, "Yes."

"There is a Mary Parsons looking for you. She's at your house, I had to calm her down by telling her you guys were okay."

"She's my sister, um. We'll go to her, thanks, she can be a handful sometimes!" unc said.

# CHAPTER 12

# AUNTY MARY

Pulling up to unc's house we could see Aunty Mary sitting in her car. When unc put the car in park, Aunty Mary exited her car. Unc opened the door to get out, then said "Lord, help us."

"It'll be fine as long as we all stay calm," Aunty Janie said, touching unc's arm.

Unc gets out of the car and is about to open the trunk when Aunty Mary walks up to him and hugs him, then says, "Sorry, Ronnie. I shouldn't have acted as I did over Jaray! I just thought..."

"Don't worry about it, Mary, I'm sorry, too. I shouldn't have acted as I did, either." They both embraced each other. A hug they both needed. While the warm breeze brushed their faces, and with their hearts healing, the resentment leaving them both, my mother said, "Do I have to sit here all day?"

"Oh, no, I have to get the wheelchair!" unc said, releasing Aunty Mary and popping the trunk.

Aunty Mary walks around to my mother's door on the passenger side back seat and opens it. She bends down and reaches in to hug my mother.

"I've missed you so much!" Aunty Mary says.

"We just saw each other a couple of weeks ago, Mary!"

"I know but I have missed you, you've been through so much these last couple of weeks I've heard. Jaray called and told me what had happened. I was so upset. I shouldn't have allowed anything between me and Ronnie. We've always been so close. I'm here now!"

Unc wheeled the wheelchair to where Aunty Mary was kneeling outside the car. Aunty Mary moved out of the way to allow unc to help my mother out and into her wheelchair.

"I have a physical therapy appointment this Friday, Ronnie, could you give me a ride? I've been meaning to ask."

"Yes, of course, I will, Barb."

"I'll wheel her, is that what you say? Or is it push?" Aunty Mary confusingly said.

"It doesn't matter," my mother replied as Aunty Janie was about to unlock the front door to the house. Opening the door, the cool air from the air conditioning racing outside. Aunty Mary pushed my mother up to the door but didn't have the strength to get the wheelchair over the transition. Unc walked up and gave it a little nudge. My mother's body bounced up and settled back down.

"Whoa! Are you guys trying to kill me?"

"No, silly!" Aunty Mary said, pushing the wheelchair positioning it by the recliner.

Aunty Charlene and Jaray pulled in just before I went inside. They had to have stopped somewhere before getting here because it took them a little longer. Inside, unc was already grabbing his remote, but the look Aunty Janie gave him, he never turned his television on. He just shook his head and walked into the kitchen. I thought about following him, maybe get myself something to drink. Then I thought, I'd like to go for a walk. With everyone locked up that were after me, I shouldn't have any problems.

"I think I'm going to go for a walk."

My mother looked at me, her worrying face locked in on me, her mouth about to say something, but she paused, then said, "Be careful!"

"Always am."

"Where are you going?" Jaray asked.

"For a walk!"

"I'll go with you, I need to get away from these white people, they are crazy, especially that one!" Jaray said, pointing to Aunty Mary.

"Oh, shut it!" Aunty Mary said. "Come give me a hug before you both run off!"

Jaray and I walked over to Aunty Mary and gave her a hug at the same time. She held us close, and said, "Joseph wanted to come but his dad needed him for a cleanup job they're doing."

Joseph is my double first cousin. He and his two sisters live back in Harken. He's just a few months older than me, only not as tough. He likes to fib a bit, too. I was kind of glad he didn't come, though, I didn't tell Aunty Mary that. We stopped bear hugging Aunty Mary and headed out the front door. Aunty Charlene had pulled Aunty Mary in for a hug as we were leaving, I could hear Aunty Charlene start crying.

"Oh God, I haven't seen you in so long!" Aunty Charlene said, her voice showing that her heart was full of joy.

"I know, Char Char! I know, it's been too long!"

# CHAPTER 13

# A FRIENDLY POOL GAME

The first place I wanted to visit was Daron's house, but I didn't know where he lived. I thought about going to the church, only figured that I wouldn't have any luck there right now anyway. So, I decided to go to Jarod's grandma's house. I may even get lucky and she could be making some food.

"Where are we going?" Jaray asked me when I started to turn on Bruce street, "I thought we could head uptown."

"Nah, I am going to Jarod's grandma's house. I don't know where Daron lives, so I can't go there."

"Okay, whatever...hey," Jaray changes the subject. "What do you think about what happened this morning, me inheriting the estate from Mr. Evanson?"

"I think you're one lucky kid!"

"You got that right; I don't even know what I now own or control."

"Guess you'll find that out on Friday?"

"Yeah, I wonder how much money I have now."

"What are you going to do with all that money? I'm sure it's a lot. Mr. Schwartz said there are well over one thousand acres of land."

"That's a lot of land."

"Yeah, there are probably cattle on quite a lot of it, I'd bet."

"So, you're telling me that I'm probably going to be a cowboy?" Jaray said, changing his walk, making himself look bow legged.

"Ha!" I said, laughing. "I could see that! You, wearing a cowboy hat, the boots, the whole nine."

"Like a Rhinestone Cowboy!" Jaray started singing.

"Oh stop!"

I could see Jarod's grandma's house a few houses down on the right with her car in the driveway. As we got closer, I could hear loud gospel music playing. A man singing something about seeing nails and hearing cries, being no stranger to pain, and walking a mile in my shoes. I remember my grandmother listening to gospel music. Only, her music was much older. Reaching the porch, the front door already open, which explains why I'd heard the music, the screen door, a faded green, slammed as Jarod came out and let it go, he had already seen me and Jaray coming upon the porch.

"Hey, Ralphie, I heard what happened. How are you?"

"I'm good. I just needed to get out and take a walk, so I thought I would come over and hang out if that's okay."

"It's okay with me, I can call Daron and we all could go for a walk!"

"Sounds good, have you met my cousin, Jaray?"

"No, nice to meet you," Jarod said, reaching out his hand to shake Jaray's, "I'm Jarod Cache."

"Jaray Morre!" Jaray said, shaking Jarod's hand.

"I'll go get the phone and come back out; my granny is playing her gospel music too loud just to irritate the neighbors," Jarod said smiling. "Be right back."

"Okay."

"I think the first thing I'm going to buy when I get my hands on some of that salt money is a mobile phone," Jaray said looking down the road. "That way I'll be available all the time."

"I wouldn't want to be available all the time," I said, looking back over my shoulder to see Jarod coming back outside. Granny's music was still playing, only a different song this time, older, something my grandma would listen to.

"Okay, let me call Daron," Jarod said dialing Daron's number, the button tone overpowering the music as he dialed the number.

I never heard a ring, but Jarod started talking, "Hey Mike, is Daron around?"

I could hear Pastor Mike talking, "Yeah, just a second, huh, he was just in here. Let me see if he is in his room. Hold on." Even though Pastor Mike wasn't talking into the phone, I could still hear him, "Daron, it's Jarod on the phone," and Daron, "Okay," Daron's voice became louder on the phone, so I guessed he'd grabbed the phone from his dad, "Hey Jarod, what's up?"

"Hey, Ralphie and his cousin are here, I think we are going to walk around, you wanna come?"

"Sure" Daron's voice fades for a second. "Meet me at my house!"

"Okay, bye!" Jarod hangs up the phone. "He wants us to meet him at his house." He looks down the road. I follow his glance. I turned back toward him and shook my head yes, Jarod then walked back through the green screen door, it creaked then it slammed again, there is just something about those old screen doors that I liked. As he put the phone up, Jaray and I stepped off the porch and started to the road, Jarod came back out jogging to us and he reached us before the slam happened again.

"Daron told me about what happened to him at your house the other day. Did they ever catch the guy?"

"Yes. There were six people involved in trying to kill me and my mother."

"Wow, just because of your skin color?"

"Actually, no, it was for money, power, and control of Evanson's Salt Company."

Jarod, obviously confused, said, "What do you have to do with the salt company?"

"That's just it, I had nothing to do with it, they just thought I did. They thought I was someone else."

"Who?"

"Me!" Jaray answered.

"You? What do you have to do with the salt company?"

"I own it!"

"Oh, stop kidding."

"No, I'm not kidding with you!"

"He's not!" I said, shaking my head and looking at Jarod.

"Really, you actually own the salt company?"

"Yes, I do now, you see, Mr. Evanson is my grandfather!"

"Really, so you and Ralphie are Mr. Evanson's grandkids?"

"No, just Jaray."

Jarod stopped walking and appeared to be lost in thought for a moment, "You are Mr. Evanson's grandson, and Mr. Evanson, who just passed away, the paper said, left you the salt company?"

"Not just the salt company, but his entire estate. All the land he owns and majority ownership in the salt company. I don't know how much just yet; I will find out more on Friday. There were some people on the board of directors for the salt company and they wanted me dead but thought Ralphie was me because the will they stole said his grandson was of negro descent and lived with a white woman. That fit Ralphie and Aunty Barb to a tee."

"Wow! That's mind-blowing," Jarod said, still walking next to me. His eyes looking at the pavement.

Jaray continued, "They wanted the three men that were after Ralphie to make it look like a KKK hate crime."

"They did a good job on that one!" Jarod said, looking at Jaray this time.

"Yeah, but they screwed up when they yelled out at the convenience store. Remember that?"

Jarod looked at me to answer my question, "That was them?"

"Yeah, Officer Madison figured it out really quick," I said before Jarod pointed out a house up the block and said, "That's Daron's house there! The one with the brown trim."

Daron was coming out the front door when I looked toward the house Jarod pointed out, "Cool, there's Daron coming out, we could have just walked up here and asked if he wanted to go, instead of calling him!"

Daron spotted us and started walking in our direction, when he met up with us, he turned to join in our walk. We didn't go to his house, though, we just continued walking. I thought about going to the Salt Palace, only because the last time we were together that's where we went, but thought against it, at least for now.

"So, how'd it all go? My dad said they caught the guys that were after you and plus some others," Daron said, stopping to pick up a small colorful rock. He glared at it then threw it ahead of us on the road.

"They caught every one of those sorry bastards. Plus, we found out that Jaray is the only grandkid of Mr. Evanson and Mr. Evanson left him everything in his will," I said, noticing the colorful rock he just threw.

"Whoa, really, that's awesome!"

"I don't know how much it's worth just yet, I'll find out more on Friday," Jaray said.

"You probably shouldn't be telling anyone. They may come after you!" Daron said out of concern.

"You're probably right, so let's just keep this between us for now, okay!" Jaray said, stopping for dramatic effect. But because he stopped, we all stopped, he then went on to say, "Let's go to the pool hall and shoot some pool." He corrected his posture and changed his accent to sound more proper, cleared his throat, and said, "Excuse me, some billiards!" Which sounded more British than anything.

"Great idea. I haven't been to the pool hall in a minute. The last time I was there, these bikers were there causing trouble and the police were called. It was fun to watch because those biker guys were hilarious," Daron said. "Although, my dad did say he didn't want me over there anymore. But that's okay, I'm not by myself this time, I have you guys to have my back."

\*\*\*

As we closed in on the pool hall, I didn't see any motorcycles outside in the parking area, but they could have walked up the road from the restaurant. I did see some bikes down there, they looked mean, all blacked out with saddlebags.

When we entered the pool hall, there were a few people playing pool, Daron went and grabbed a pool stick off the wall and Jarod put quarters in the slot and made the balls jump with joy. You could hear them falling from their holding place. Jaray pulled the triangle rack out of the side and started pulling the balls up to the top of the table and racking them up.

"Who has the first game?" Daron asked.

"I'll go!" Jaray said, I'm already racking the balls.

"It's my quarters!" Jarod said.

"Well, I'll just have to buy you out then."

"There you go!" I said, talking to Jaray because he was already letting the money he hasn't even got yet go to his head.

"Shut up!" Jaray said, grabbing a pool stick, "I'm only kidding around!"

"Let's go, I'll bust!" Daron said.

Jaray, chalking his hand and the pool stick, said, "Go ahead, buster!"

Daron laid the pool stick on the table. Lining the stick up with the cue ball to make his bust, he moved the stick forward a little too fast and hit the cue ball just under the bottom, we watched the ball jump over the racked balls and off the table. Jarod chased the ball under the next table.

"He just tried to kill me," I said, joking around, pointing at Daron.

Jarod handed the cue ball to Jaray and Jaray set up his shot to bust the rack. He lined up the stick with the cue ball and took a deep breath, then sent the cue ball into the racked balls, hitting the yellow ball, number one perfectly, sending the balls everywhere. The green ball, number six, came to his side of the table and slowed down to a stop while the purple striped number twelve ball fell into the corner pocket.

"Got my stripes," Jaray said, gearing up for his second shot, called his shot. "Orange striped thirteen corner pocket." Then he sent the cue ball into the orange striped thirteen and it barely moved.

Daron laughed and walked over to where the cue ball stopped on the table, "Lined his shot and pushed the cue ball into the maroon number seven ball, to no avail.

"You didn't even call your shot, dufus!" Jaray said.

"I wasn't going to call anything because I was just spreading everything out!"

"You can't do that, dummy!" Jarod said.

Daron, talking over him, "I know what I'm doing!"

"Watch this!" Jaray said, lining up his shot going after the blue striped number ten. "Ten-ball one o'clock!" He shot and the ten-ball sunk into the corner pocket. He went after the brown number fifteen next and sunk it into the side pocket, then scratched on his next shot.

"Okay, scratcher! "Daron said, grabbing the cue ball, centering it on the end. He then settled his stick on the side of the table shooting for the red three-ball and shot it in the far corner pocket.

"Now you are giving me a run for my money!" Jaray said, watching Daron set up his next shot, the yellow number one ball. Daron makes his shot the yellow ball hits the side and then smacks into the black eight-ball sending it into the side pocket.

"No!" Daron shouts, closing his eyes throwing his pool stick on the table!"

"That's game, big baby!" Jaray says, laughing with Jarod, and I. "Who's next?"

"Jarod, you can go next," I said, which gets him to grab the pool stick Daron threw on the table.

"I'm not good at all, so you'll have to take it easy on me, Jaray!"

"Let me think about that...uh, no!"

"Alright then!"

"I think you may be getting played." I said to Jaray, "Jarod is probably a pro!"

"He's good!" Daron adds.

Jarod racks the balls and centers them, pulls the triangle rack off the table and Jaray sends the cue ball to do its job. Balls go all over the table, hitting the sides and bouncing into each other, the red three ball into black eight, sending it into the corner pocket.

"Let's try this again," Jaray said. "I'll re-spot the ball, since I didn't scratch.

"Okay," Jarod said, pulling the eight-ball out of the pocket and handing it to Jaray.

Jaray shot again, sending two solid colored balls into the middle pocket. Jarod made a shot and didn't sink any striped balls. Jaray stepped up to make another shot and missed the solid green and hit the cue ball into the eight-ball pocketing it. "What the crap?" Jaray says, as he threw his pool stick onto the table.

"That was too easy," Jarod said. "Ralphie, you're next!"

"I think I'll pass on this one and get the next!"

"Forget that, let's get out of here! We are not having any luck!" Jaray says. "Plus, I want something to eat."

"Yeah, let's go!" I added.

I don't know why but I was bored. I didn't want to play pool. I didn't want to be alone. I wanted answers that I know Daron, Jarod, and Jaray couldn't help me with. I didn't know who to talk to about it. My mother has problems of her own and I didn't want to bother her about it, at least not until she's finished her physical therapy, or maybe even walking again. I couldn't talk to unc because he would talk to my mother. Aunty Janie would listen, but she would tell unc and you know what happens then. So, I'm limited. Maybe I could talk with Pastor Mike, but I don't want him to think differently of me. I've only just made friends with his son.

"Ralphie, are you okay?" Jaray says. "You look lost, snap out of it, I thought we were leaving."

"Maybe you should talk with my dad about what happened to you, he could help. He helps all kinds of people with their personal problems," Daron suggested.

I looked at Daron, he was reading my mind. I shook it off, and said, "Yeah, I think I might do that."

"Okay, I'll tell him to put you on his schedule and he'll call you and let you know when and what time."

"Thanks," I said, as we walked out of the pool hall into a darkening sky.

"I think we should get home or something, looks like it might start raining," Jarod said, looking up at the sky.

"Yeah," Jaray agreed.

# CHAPTER 14

# A TYPEWRITER AND A GIRL

My mother was sipping on a cup of coffee from her Marlboro cup, the red logo with black letters under it spelling out Marlboro. She sat at the kitchen table, a cigarette sat in the ashtray, smoke chasing itself reaching for the ceiling.

"Good morning, mom."

"Good morning, Ralphie."

I go over to the cabinet and grab a cup to pour myself some coffee, I turn the sugar container upside down into my cup and watch the coffee soak it up, then added the creamer just the way I like it. Some sugar with a dash of creamer and a little coffee.

"You want some coffee with that sugar?" my mother asked, jokingly.

"You know it!"

I brought my coffee over to the table and pulled up a seat. As I was taking a sip my mother looked at me, took a drag off her cigarette, then put it back into the ashtray. Blowing the smoke from her lungs toward the opened window to keep it from going into my face, she says, "I have physical therapy this morning, your Aunt Mary is going to take me, are you going to your uncle's?"

"I don't know, doesn't Jaray have that thing today?"

"Yeah, but you could go with, he would want you to."

"I may just stay here and watch some TV."

"Well, I have physical therapy and then I have to enroll you into school. It starts in just over a week, August 5th. Are you ready for school?"

"Yeah, I actually am ready, I want to see what it's like being the only black kid in school."

"Oh, quit it!"

"No, I'm serious, Daron says that there are no black kids, there are just white kids, a handful of Mexicans and two Asians, both female."

Blowing her cigarette smoke toward the window again she said, "Two Asian girls huh? I bet they're both cute!"

"Well, Daron did say…"

"I knew it!" my mother said, smiling.

Aunty Mary walked in the front door without knocking, "Good morning, sunshine!"

"Good morning," my mother and I said in unison.

"Are you ready to go?" Aunty Mary asked, walking over to the kitchen table taking a seat next to me.

"Ralphie, since when do you drink coffee?"

"Since now, Aunty Mary! Since when are you so nosy?"

"Since forever!"

We both started laughing, my mother putting her cigarette out joined us, "I'm ready!" Smoke fighting to stay inside while the window pulled the smoke toward it.

"Ralphie, go get that folder beside my bed. I need it to enroll you."

"Okay," I said, setting my cup down after taking a sip. I get up from the table and make my way to her room. The door closed, I opened the door and walked over to the side table where I saw a folder. I picked it up and just out of curiosity, I opened it. Inside were my birth certificate, social security card, my transcripts from Harken, a GPA of 3.8, and a letter from my old principal.

To whom it may concern:

Ralph Parsons is an extraordinary young man. As his principal at Harken Booker T. Schools, I have witnessed his good attitude among his peers and his growth as a student. He has been a consistently good student earning the best of grades and is among the top students in his class. He is one of the best learners and at times a great teacher, as Mrs. Irwin's assistant, his English teacher. Ralph has volunteered for our afterschool programs throughout the last few years. I hope that you will accept him with great honor.

I also hope this recommendation would be considered to help you understand that Ralph Parsons is a leader and has become a role model to many students who do not hesitate to ask him questions. He has excelled here at Harken Booker T. Schools with great honors and with a 3.8 GPA.

Sincerely,

Mr. Michael A. Carter (Mac)

Principal, Harken Booker T. Schools

I miss Mac. He was a great mentor to me. Maybe I should have called him during all this madness. He may have dealt with racism in his past, too. I thought about the reasons why I've stayed and volunteered after school, and it was because I didn't want to fight with those wannabe gangsters.

"Ralphie, what's taking you so long in there?"

"Just reading, mom," I said, putting the letter back into the folder. I walked back into the kitchen and Aunty Mary was unlocking my mother's wheelchair.

"We're about to get going!" Aunty Mary said, wheeling my mother's chair into the living room.

"Ralphie, go down to your Uncle's until your Aunt Mary brings me home!"

"Okay, mom," I said, watching them leave the porch and head to Aunty Mary's car.

"Do you want me to help you into the car, mom?"

"No, we can do it, thank you, though!"

I watched them get in the car and drive off down the road, heading south, then turn right on Main Street, heading to the hospital clinic. I then looked north, remembering what had happened to me a couple of weeks ago. River Road has been a nightmare, I'm not even sure I want to live here anymore. Maybe I can talk mom into finding another house, not on River Road, though. Feeling my neck, the roughness of the scarring from the rope. I swallowed hard, trying to put it out of my mind. How does one do that, after suffering something like that? It all started with my Aunty Charlene because she was a black female, Leroy Evanson raped her while his friends watched and cheered him on. It's not her fault that happened to her, none of this is. It's not any of our faults, that any of this happened to us. Jaray cannot help who his father is, and we cannot help what our skin color is. God creates everyone differently, uniquely, and to his liking. We were attacked this time because someone wanted power and money. They thought they would kill us and make it look like it was racism, however, they didn't think the FBI would be called, but that's what happens when there is a hate crime. They didn't have any power over us. I remember something my grandmother told me; she said the bible says that every soul is subject unto the higher powers. For there is no power but of God: the powers that be are ordained by God. The racist, murderers, rapists, and the like are the devil's salt. The Devil's Salt on River Road.

\*\*\*

When unc let me in after I'd knocked and rang the doorbell about a billion times, he was still in his pajamas.

"I thought you and Jaray were going to the courthouse this morning."

"He asked his mother to go, I didn't want to be there and get in the way of them bonding."

"I see. Maybe I won't ask to go then."

"Nah, let them have their time, we don't know how long it will last."

"How long what will last?" Jaray asked, coming around the corner from the hallway.

"Oh, nothing... are you wearing that to the courthouse?"

"No. I just threw my pants in the dryer; these shorts are so that I don't embarrass you!" Jaray said, laughing.

"Shoot, boy. I have your embarrassment," unc said, before going into the hall, back to his room.

"What's up Ralphie. Do you want to go with us?"

"Nah, I'm going to go to Daron's, his dad hasn't called me so I'm going to see if Daron forgot to tell him."

"You know you can talk to me, whenever you want!"

"Yeah, I just don't know what it is I need to say. I'm confused, I don't know what to do."

"It's all going to be good. After the meeting this morning, I'm going to be making some major changes in all our lives. Stick with ya boy, you feel me?"

"You know I got your back anytime, Jaray, for the rest of my life." Jaray came over to give me a hug.

"My mom hasn't made it yet and it's almost time for us to leave," Jaray said, releasing me from our hug.

"I thought she was staying here," I said to Jaray as he was looking out the window, bringing the blind down as if his eyes were too big and he couldn't see unless it was open at least a foot.

"JARAY!" unc yelled. "Don't you break my blinds. You know better than that."

"Sorry unc, it's just mom hasn't made it yet."

"She'll be here, quit worrying."

"Unc, you know I worry about her; she can be unstable sometimes."

"Yeah, I know," unc said as someone knocked on the door. Jaray swung it open and found his mother standing there.

"Are you ready?"

"Yes," he said, smiling from ear to ear. "I just looked out and didn't see your car."

"It's parked a little way up. I didn't want to risk stepping out into a puddle when I got out of the car," she said, looking back at the muddy driveway.

"Ralphie, are you going with us?" Aunt Charlene asked.

I looked over at unc and then back at her, "Nah, I'm going to a friend's house, I have to talk to his dad."

"Okay, suit yourself," she said as she and Jaray walked out the door and toward her car parked up the road a bit.

***

While my mother was doing her physical therapy and Jaray was learning about everything he owns now, I walked over to Daron's. Their driveway was paved, so I didn't have to worry about walking in any mud puddles. I reached his door and knocked, then noticed there was a doorbell, so I rang the doorbell. Seconds later a young girl answered, I thought maybe she could be Daron's sister. "Could I help you?" the young lady said, looking me in the eyes then glazed at my neck.

"Um, is Daron here?" I said nervously.

"Yes, hold on," she turned and yelled. "Daron, some boy is at the door for you!"

"He's coming, come in!" the young lady said.

"Thanks!"

"You're very welcome," she said, walking toward the kitchen.

I heard Daron coming down the stairs, when he reached the bottom, he did a what's up motion with his head, and voiced it, "What's up Ralphie?"

"Hey, I didn't know you had a sister?"

"I don't, that's my stupid cousin, Alura," Daron said, waving her off as if she was nothing but trouble.

"Alura, huh, like the comics, the mother of Supergirl?"

"Ralphie, you have a crush on her?" Daron said, grabbing my shoulder. "You have been hit by what the Italians call the thunderbolt!"

"What? The thunderbolt?"

"Yeah, it's when love strikes someone like lightning. It's so obvious, Ralphie!"

"Whatever!"

"Come on, let's go to my room," Daron said, walking back up the stairs.

My heart was pounding as I tried to peek into the kitchen, trying to see if I could get another look at Alura before going up the stairs. I didn't see anyone, the kitchen was empty and quiet, except for the kettle, sitting on a blue flame sweating, the whistle seconds away from screaming. I was a few steps up the stairs when I heard the whistling, and someone pulled the kettle off the burner. I fought the urge to go back and take a peek. A thunderbolt, I thought to myself.

Daron, interrupting my thoughts, said, "Ralphie, what are you doing?"

I hadn't realized I stopped midway up the stairs, "Nothing."

I followed Daron up the stairs and into his room, Jarod was sitting at Daron's desk, typing on a typewriter. He turned and said hello.

"What's up, Jarod, what are you doing?" I asked, interested in the typewriter. I thought about how much easier it would be for me to write my story, instead of using the pen and paper I have at home.

"Ralphie likes Alura!" Daron said to Jarod, "Called her his Supergirl!"

"I did not!"

"Oh yeah, you can have her, she is a headache!" Jarod said, rolling his eyes.

"A headache," I said, imagining her giving me a headache, at this moment my heart was aching to see her again.

"Yeah, she is tough, she's not afraid to take on anyone," Daron said. "She's just here helping my mom make some food for the revival tonight at the church. You should come!"

"I don't know, I've got things going on later with Jaray," I said, thinking about Jaray and how happy he is going to be with his newfound wealth.

"Well, if you change your mind, Alura will be there, too!" Daron said, giving me a little shove.

I caught my balance and said without thinking I said, "She will? I mean…"

"See I told ya!" Daron said looking at Jarod, who then said while chuckling, "He really does like her!"

"Nah, I'll stop kidding around about Alura, but you're welcome to ask her out if you want," Daron said, his body shaking with mirth.

"Hey, well, I came by to see if you talked to your dad," I said, changing the subject, even though I wanted to know more about Alura.

"Yeah, he just said to have you come to him and he'll just stop whatever he is doing and talk with you."

"Okay, is he here now?"

"No, he had to go to Dallas because some preacher is coming in to preach tonight. And he is picking him up at the airport."

"Oh, okay. Maybe I'll catch him later," I said, looking over at Jarod typing on the typewriter. "I'd like to have one of those. It would beat writing with a pen and paper."

"Yeah, it's nice," Jarod said, still typing.

"What are you writing?"

"It's a sermon for church tonight, I'm going to be a guest preacher for the youth service."

"Oh, that's cool."

"Yeah, dad likes to let us do that occasionally. He says it helps bring other kids closer to God because they get to think deeper about what they would say to the other kids about God."

"I'd like to borrow that typewriter to write about what happened to me. You know, my story. Could I borrow it?"

"Yeah, as soon as Jarod is done."

"Okay, thanks."

"Don't mention it, I don't use it anyway. I got it for Christmas a couple of years ago and Jarod is the only person that uses it."

"You don't write?"

"No. I'd rather just make it up as I go. Mom and dad wanted me to write but it's just not me."

"I'm done, you want to hear it?" Jarod asked, pulling the last paper from the typewriter.

"I'll hear it tonight. So no, not right now!" Daron said, putting a stop to Jarod preaching his sermon too early.

"Ralphie?" Jarod asked.

"If I go tonight, I'll hear it then. I just came by to see if Daron talked to his dad," I turned to Daron. "So, I'll just catch him later sometime. I need to get back to my uncle's house to see if Jaray has made it back yet."

"Okay, I'll tell dad you came by and wanted to talk, here," Daron walked over to the typewriter and put it in the case. "Take this, write your story!"

"Thanks."

Daron went and opened the door after handing me the typewriter and we all started down the stairs. I heard people talking, both obviously female, one sounded much older than the other. The other must have been Alura. Maybe I would get my chance to set my eyes on her again. As we hit the last step, I looked into the kitchen and no one was in there.

"Where are you guys going?" Alura asked. I turned to where her voice came from and there she was, looking at me, she glanced at my neck and then up at my eyes.

"Noneya," Daron said, putting his hand in Alura's face. She grabbed it and bent his fingers back, it didn't bother him, but it sickened me. "That doesn't hurt!" he finished, and she let his hand go.

"I'm going to my uncle's house. My cousin should be there, and he's got some good news I'd like to hear about," I said, looking at Alura, how her green eyes widened when I spoke. Her hair was in a ponytail, but I could tell it was brown, a few strings laid on the right side of her face.

"Are all of you going?" she asked.

"Maybe, maybe not!" Jarod said, wanting in on the action.

"Shut up, Jarod," Alura said, shoving him then looking at me again. "Well, if you two go then I want to go, too. I'm done helping Aunt Molly, so I'm free to go!"

"Mom, is she really done helping you?" Daron asked, peeking his head into the living room.

"Yes," Daron's mom said, he turned and opened the front door, we all walked outside onto the porch. The sun was beating down and the heat hit us like a wind breeze.

"Man, it's hot out," Jarod said, feeling the humid July air.

"Yes, it is," I agreed. "Well guys, I'll see ya. Thanks for letting me borrow the typewriter," I said, which brought Alura's eyes to just notice that I had the typewriter in my left hand.

"What are you doing with the typewriter?"

"I'm writing my story. I already started on pen and paper, but I thought the typewriter would be better, so Daron was nice enough to loan it to me."

"What are you writing? I'm Alura, by the way."

"I'm Ralph, uh Ralphie."

"Well, nice to meet you, Ralph, uh Ralphie!"

"Nice to meet ya, too!" I said, nervously.

"So, what are you writing?"

"I'm writing about what recently happened to me," I said, feeling my neck with my right hand, the typewriter weighing down the other. We then just stood there looking at each other. No words. We probably both stopped breathing for a moment.

"Uh, hello! Earth to Ralphie and Alura," Daron said, breaking our eye contact, forcing us to try and hide our attraction for each other.

"I'll see you guys… Alura," I said, looking at Alura.

"You guys are not going with Ralphie?" Alura asked, she turned and started looking at Jarod and Daron.

"No. I have to get home," Jarod said.

"You go if you want!" Daron said to Alura.

I could tell she wanted to go but she held back, "No, I have to get home, too. Bye Ralphie," she said, barely lifting her hand to wave as if she was disappointed in herself for not revealing that she wanted to go.

"See ya," I said, my peace sign matching the ones Jaray gives me all the time. I begin walking toward unc's house, my thoughts still on Alura. I thought about going to church tonight just to see her again, or maybe even ask her out. But I still wanted to hang out with Jaray and see what he was told by his lawyer. I thought of my mother and her physical therapy and that she would jump with joy from hearing that I like a girl.

# CHAPTER 15

# FRIDAY NIGHT REVIVAL

With Alura still on my mind, I walked into unc's house and sat down on his couch. I set the typewriter down beside me. Unc, sitting back down in his recliner, since he just got up to let me in, he looked over at me and said, "What's got you, Ralphie? You seem a little off!"

"I met a girl," I said, still trying to calm my heart.

"You met a girl? It's about time, I was beginning to worry about you!"

"She is beautiful," I said, ignoring what he said.

"What's her name?"

"Alura!" I said. "My Supergirl!"

"Supergirl?" unc said, chuckling. Turning the volume back up on the television talking about sports, I didn't care though, all I saw was Alura.

"Is Jaray back yet?"

"No, they haven't made it back yet," Aunty Janie said, walking into the living room joining me on the couch. "What's this for, Ralphie?" she continued, looking at the typewriter.

"I was wondering that myself," unc said. "But Ralphie distracted me by talking about a girl he'd just met."

"You met a girl, Ralphie? What's her name?"

"Her name is Alura, his Supergirl!" unc answered, sarcastically.

"The typewriter is for me to write my story," I said, putting my hand on my neck and feeling the tissue, still a little sore and tough, but healing nicely.

"Oh, that would be good," Aunty Janie said. "I love to read."

"No, you don't!" unc said, shaking his head.

"Oh, hush it, yes I do!" Aunty Janie countered.

"Are you going to put that girl in your story, Ralph?" unc asked, picking on me now.

"I don't know. I just met her. When do you think Jaray will be back?" I asked, hoping to change the subject, even though I couldn't get my mind off of Alura.

"Hard to tell," unc said. "They may even have gone out to celebrate."

"They wouldn't go without all of us," I said. "You know that!"

"He's right, Ron," Aunty Janie said as the front door opened. "They wouldn't do that."

Coming in the door overhearing Aunty Janie, Jaray said, "Who wouldn't do what?" His smile couldn't leave his face no matter how hard he tried to hide it.

"You guys are back. I was just saying you wouldn't go out and celebrate without us." Aunty Janie said, standing to hug Jaray and Aunty Charlene. They embraced each other and then sat down. Everyone sat quietly waiting to hear the results of what was now owned by Jaray.

"Well?" unc asked.

"Well, it seems that I own fifty-six percent, majority, of the Evanson's Salt Company. The land I own is all over Grayson. Five hundred acres is just north of town, mostly wooded. The Saline river goes right through the property. Turns out, the last mile of River Road, all of Ferry Road, and Crain's Ferry all belongs to me now."

"Where is the other land?" Aunty Janie asked, sitting on the edge of her seat.

"One hundred acres is where the salt mine is, there are some buildings downtown, the bank building is one of them, the Salt Palace, the property which the hardware store is located on is also mine. There are forty-three houses I now own, including your house Ralphie."

"What, that's awesome," I said. "I have to tell my mom, although, I think I want to move off of River Road, though!"

"That's totally understandable," Aunty Charlene said. "I wouldn't want to be on that road either. Too much hate has traveled River Road."

"I'll tell you what we could do," Jaray said, standing, placing his right hand on his head, pondering. "We could… because I own the properties just before your house, we could fence off the whole entire property, all five hundred acres and put a gate on River Road, to keep traffic and people off as best as we can. How does that sound?"

"I like it," I said, with excitement.

Jaray sat down, "I think I will set up a new company, a management company for all my properties and interests, I may even call it Some Morre Companies, I'm just kidding. It'll be JaMorre Properties."

"That's a great name, Jaray!" Aunty Charlene said.

"Yeah, I want all you guys to work for JaMorre Properties, in one way or the another. Aunty Barb, too."

"Well, we'll have to sit down and plan, make a business plan, before we just jump into it," unc said, adjusting himself in his seat. "First things first, setting up a board of directors and what their director positions will be used for. But we'll get to all that, soon enough."

"We've already set up a bank account for mom and I, so that we can get her the help she needs. Until she is clean for six months or more, Mr. Schwartz will have to approve all withdrawals. I'm not old enough to do so, at this moment," Jaray said, shrugging his shoulders.

"It'll be fine, Jaray, I am going to put all that behind me and work to keep our relationship, as I should have many years ago. I love you, and I hope you can forgive me," Aunty Charlene said between tears. Jaray walked over and sat beside her and gave her a hug.

A knock at the front door startled us all. Unc got up to answer the door but it swung open before he could reach it. We all could see through the doorway the culprit, Aunty Mary, standing there behind my mother and her wheelchair. My mother wheeled herself through the door and Aunty Mary followed her in.

"Physical therapy is done for today at least, and it was promising. I could actually move my legs a bit, not enough to walk, though... not just yet anyway. But it will come, I can feel it!" my mother said.

"That's great news!" Aunty Janie said, wiping a tear from her eye. She walked over to my mother, bent down, and gave her a hug, Aunty Charlene did the same.

"That's awesome mom, I'm so happy! Now if we could get you to put the cigarettes down."

"There's another time and place for that, Ralphie," my mother said. "I have to get through this therapy and see about finding another job, no offense, Jaray. I know you are the new owner of the salt company."

"None taken; however, we've been talking, and I'm starting another company to manage all the properties and interests I own, JaMorre Properties, Inc., we are going to set up a board of directors soon. I want you to be a part of it, Aunty Barb!"

"Let me think about it."

"Mom, he also owns our house now, too."

"Is that right? You still going to charge your Aunty rent?"

"Well, actually, we were talking about you guys moving out of that house and off of River Road. I have a plan for all the property out there."

"The property out there? Are you telling me that you own Crain's Ferry?" my mother asked. "Something needs to be done about that place and the creeping hook road."

"I am thinking about fencing it all off and putting up a gate just before your house to try to keep people out," Jaray said. "Many bad things have happened down River Road and I feel now that I have the means to change it, I'm going to something about it."

"That's good news!" Aunty Mary said. "Do I get to sit on the board of directors, too?"

"Yes, Aunty Mary, you sure do, we also may have some interest in Harken, and you can be in control of that there," Jaray said hugging Aunty Mary. "Plus, that would give me a reason to come to see you, crazy folks."

"Don't be funny!" Aunty Mary said, laughing, pulling away from Jaray's hug then pulling him back for a bigger hug.

"You know guys, let's go celebrate," unc suggested.

"Yeah, let's do that, it'll be my treat!" Jaray said. "I'm driving, no questions asked. Except for who is going to let me drive their vehicle because I personally don't own one, yet."

Everyone laughed and started gathering what they needed to take with them, "Where are we going to go?"

"To…" I said before I was interrupted by unc, "No Mexican food, please."

"To Missy's Bar and Grill, I have never eaten there, and I hear it's delicious," I said after I was allowed to get a word in.

"Missy's it is!" Jaray agreed.

"Then we can talk about Ralphie's new girlfriend," unc teased.

"She's not my girlfriend," I said, even though I wished she were.

"Ralphie, has a girlfriend?" my mother questioned, looking over at unc.

"She's all he keeps talking about, Alura this, Alura that!"

"That's not true," I said, shoving unc back, playfully.

"Alura, what a beautiful name. I bet she is beautiful, too," my mother said, dreamingly.

"She's not my girlfriend but I do like her, and I might ask her out, tonight at church if we're done before the church is over."

"I'll make sure you get there," unc said, putting his hand on my shoulder guiding me out the door following Aunty Mary and my mom. Jaray and Aunty Charlene followed behind them and Aunty Janie locked the door behind us all.

"So, I guess I'm driving mom's car then, right mom?" Jaray said, talking to Aunty Charlene.

"Sure."

"I want to drive!" I exclaimed.

"Not a chance," unc said, gripping his keys before unlocking the door to Aunty Janie's car. "The last time you were in my car, it got smashed into…. I'm sorry I shouldn't be kidding about that."

"It's all good, unc, all in fun," I said, patting him on the back before getting into the back seat of Aunty Janie's car. My mother and Aunty Mary got in on the other side.

\*\*\*

After we celebrated, Jaray dropped me off at church in Aunty Charlene's car. "You want me to come to pick you up when it's over?" he asked.

"No, I'll walk back," I said, hoping I could talk Alura into walking with me.

"Okay, just be careful!"

"Look at you, being all adult-like and stuff," I said.

"Shut up punk!" Jaray said, driving off.

The parking lot at the church was packed, people were standing outside and just inside the doors, I could see Pastor Mike, greeting church members as they walked in. I figured I could use this time to talk to him. I got in line and made my way to the door; I could see Daron inside talking with Jarod. I thought for a moment to just go and hang out with them before the service started but then Pastor Mike said, "Ralphie, nice to see you again," he glanced at my neck and then to my face. "How are you?"

"I'm good, I wanted to talk to you!"

"Okay, uh, let's go to my office," he said, then motioned to another associate pastor to take his spot. We walked in his office and he offered me a soda as we sat down at his desk, "What's going on, Ralphie, how can I help you?"

I opened the soda, took a sip and then said, "Well, I really don't know. I just needed someone to talk to. I don't feel like talking to my mother would help, at least not help her, so I haven't mentioned anything."

"That's understandable, she's been through a lot as well as you have, but maybe talking to her could be beneficial for the both of you!"

"Maybe, but I don't want her to worry. I just don't understand why I was feeling a certain way, but today, today has been great."

"How have you been feeling lately?"

"Sad and lonely," I said a little too quickly. "I mean… I thought I was going to lose my mother and now she is in a wheelchair. Although, she is getting closer to walking."

"That's great news!" he said.

I continued, "I have this ugly scar on my neck that everyone seems to look at when they see me, it's embarrassing sometimes."

"I understand, and the reason I say I understand is that I, too, am guilty of looking. It's something you can't really hide unless you put something over it, maybe wearing a turtleneck shirt would help until you could get a doctor to help you heal it."

"I could do that, but at the same time, it's a story to tell. One that I think people need to hear. Money and power are recipes for disaster."

"Yes, First Timothy six-ten says, the love of money is the root of all evil," Pastor Mike said, pulling out his bible, turning to First Timothy.

"My grandmother used to say that."

"You know, I knew your grandparents."

"I haven't met many around here that hadn't," I said.

"Yeah, they were great people. Everyone loved the Morre's."

"Yup sure did and I still do."

"That's right."

"Thanks for taking the time to talk to me," I said, standing up.

"Where are you going? Is there anything else?"

"Well, I don't know. I just… felt like I couldn't fix what's going on. But maybe I can write my story and work things out."

"Yes, I heard that you borrowed Daron's typewriter, he never used it. I hope that helps and I'd like to read your story sometime."

"Yeah, the typewriter is at my uncle's house. I have to remember to get it before I go home. I'd like to write my story this weekend if I can."

"We all need to express ourselves somehow, some people do it evilly though and that's not good for anyone. The devil likes to use some to do his bidding, unfortunately, you and your mother were targeted by those devilish characters and almost lost your lives. We are chosen to be the salt of the earth and if we lose our saltiness, we become worthless and should be thrown out. Those that do not get thrown out, don't spread any good, just evil," Pastor Mike said, leaning in on his desk to get closer to me to show me how serious the knowledge he preached was for my benefit.

"Yeah, you said that during your sermon that Sunday."

"You remember?"

"Yes, I had thought about it a lot, that was one reason we decided to visit the Salt Palace."

"I see… sometimes, we have to go through trials and tribulations for the greater good. It sounds like that's what happened here. You coming to church and hearing me preach about the salt of the earth, brought you to the Salt Palace. All-knowing God, planned for you to be there, God used you for the greater good of your family."

"And that may be my real problem. I feel used!" I said, sadly, sitting back in my chair, laying my head on the headrest. I tried to catch the tear before it dropped from my eye, but many followed after it. Pastor Mike pushed his chair back and got up and to give me a tissue from his desk and he hugged me.

"God loves you, Ralphie. He loves all of us. The things we go through here on earth are temporary," he said as I shook my head in understanding. "Let me pray for you, Ralphie, then we can go see the guests' preachers."

"Okay!"

He began, "Father God, as your children we come to you. We ask that your will be done. We ask for strength and understanding of your will, so we won't suffer in our thoughts. We ask that you bless us as you carry out your will in our lives. Ralphie is having trouble, Lord and we ask that you help him become strong in your word so that he can help those around him be strong. In your name, Jesus, amen."

"Amen."

"Ralphie, anytime you need to talk, no matter what time it is, you call me, find me, wake me, it doesn't matter, you understand?"

"Yes sir."

"Okay, let's go listen to some preaching."

We walked out of his office and Jarod was in the pulpit, preaching his sermon. I stood in the back, so as not to disturb anyone. Pastor Mike stood beside me. We both listened together as Jarod preached his sermon.

"That's why the Lord brought us together tonight, to hear his word in a different light. When I was asked to preach tonight, I was honored, but then I had remembered something I was taught, and that is that I'm just a vessel and I should only let God use me to spread his word to those who can relate to me and to those who cannot. We have flavor and if the flavor was to disappear it should be thrown away. That's what happened to those flavorless people that caused so much chaos in the past few weeks, to my friend and his family, but they were thrown out. God kept the good salt and threw out the bad. I thank him for that, not only because I live here, but because God walks among us. You see, God knew their evil plan all along, and he had a plan, too. His plan and his will, will always prevail. Let us pray, Father, thank you for bringing us together tonight, and using me as your vessel to share your word with everyone here. I ask that it finds itself into someone's heart tonight, God, and I pray you allow it to grow. I thank you again, Lord, in Jesus's name, amen."

"Amen," I say joining the crowd, clapping. Pastor Mike went up to the pulpit and hugged Jarod. I'm sure he whispered to him, good job and told him he did an outstanding job preaching. At least I thought he did a great job.

Pastor Mike took the reins and introduced the next guest speaker, Billy Graham. Jarod came over to me and asked, "What did you think?"

"It was great, actually more than great. Thank you!"

"Don't thank me, thank God!" Jarod said with his hand on my shoulder. He then pulled me in, and we hugged. I thanked him again anyway.

"You're welcome, Ralphie!" he said as we walked to the dining room where most of the kids were. I later learned about Billy Graham and regret not staying in there to hear him preach, although I did hear some and thought the guy was good. I heard he brought the crowd I saw that was lined up and brought over half of them to Jesus that night.

In the dining room, I spotted Alura. I wasn't going to miss the opportunity to ask her to go for a walk with me. I walked over to her as she was making a sandwich. She put mayonnaise, lettuce, tomatoes, and pickles on it, grabbed some ham and turkey, and put it between the buns. Then she looked at me, but this time didn't glance at my neck.

"Hey," I said.

"Hey, Ralphie. Nice to see you again!" she said, then took a bite from her sandwich, a piece of lettuce dropped to the floor. "Oops."

"Would you like to go for a walk with me?" I asked. "Well, after you eat, of course."

"Sure," she said with a mouthful of her sandwich.

"Are you going to eat, Ralphie?" Daron asked, walking over to me holding a plate and pointing to the others.

"Nah, I already ate before I came. We celebrated Jaray's inheritance."

"All right then, how did that go?"

"It went great," I said, sharing my attention with both him and Alura.

"That's good," Daron said filling his plate with everything on the table. We all went and sat down, and I watched as they ate. Jarod brought us all drinks, even though Daron had already grabbed himself a drink.1

# CHAPTER 16

# REPORTING TO SCHOOL AND A FRIENDLY GUEST

The halls in the school were crowded like the schools in Harken, the kids stared as I walked to my first class. Luckily, I wore a white turtleneck and a brown vest, I knew they weren't looking at me because of my neck, so it could have only been because I was the new kid, but it is the first day of school, there are several new kids. So, it's possible that the only reason they were staring at me was because I'm not a white kid. I was the only black kid in school, especially since Jaray didn't start today. He said he would probably continue being homeschooled by unc.

I couldn't even find my class at first, but I spotted Alura. She came up to me and we walked down the hall together, "What's your first class?" she asked.

"History, Mr. Gevins."

"Me too."

"Cool, you can show me where it is, then."

"Come on," she said, pulling me, and I followed behind like a little puppy dog. When we made it to history class, Alura walked in first and no one batted an eye. The room was noisy with everyone talking around the room. After I walked in, the chatter slowed, the room quieted a decibel or two, and everyone looked, even Mr. Gevins did a doubletake. I was thinking, hello, I'm Ralphie, and I'm black. What is this, whites-anonymous? Of course, I didn't say any of that out loud, but if I had maybe it would have made everyone laugh. A kid shouldn't be this nervous on his first day of school.

I took my seat by Alura and everyone started chatting again, even louder than before. Mr. Gevins sat at his desk going through a book. There's probably a lesson in the workbook that he's getting ready to teach us. I could see similar books stacked on the table in the corner.

Looking around the room I identified some potential bullies, made a note to stay clear of them. I didn't need any more trouble with white people. I saw the two Asian girls, they are pretty, but they're no Alura. I look over at Alura and she was doing the same, checking out everyone in the room. The Asian girls came over to her and they were all talking as if they were best friends. Which kind of made me jealous.

Mr. Gevins stood up and walked over to begin writing on the chalkboard. The class starts to quiet down the kids went back to their desks. If we were at Harken, the kids would have continued to be noisy, running around the room during class time and the teacher would have just ignored them. Mr. Gevins asked some nerdy looking white kids to help him hand out the workbooks that were on the corner table. It wasn't very thick, but it was a new book. Harken books weren't new, and they had writing all over them, nothing to help with being book smart, only street smart.

In my next class, which is English, Daron, Jarod, and Alura were there and all of them sat around me. I felt at home in their company. We joked around while watching the teacher, Ms. Sanders write sentences on the chalkboard. As I watched the sentences form, I started daydreaming about mom walking again and us moving into a new house, not on River Road, even though my house was just down the road from the school. I daydreamed about Alura and I hanging out after school, going for a walk like we did that Friday at church, when I had asked her to go out with me and she agreed. I thought about Jaray and how he could do good things with the money he'd inherited.

"Ralphie, come back to us, Earth to Ralphie," Daron said, shaking me.

"What?"

"You were staring into space, what are you thinking about?"

"Oh, nothing, really."

"Aluurra!" Jarod said, making Alura's name sound like it had too many letter r's."

"So, what if I was?" I asked smiling, looking at Alura. She smiled back and then Ms. Sanders turned and shushed us.

"Yeah Daron, put a sock in it," I said and everyone in the class laughed including Ms. Sanders.

***

After school, Alura and I walked home, to my house first since it was closer. When we walked in my mother was sitting at the kitchen table, smoking a cigarette. She put it out, "Ralphie, come here."

I walked toward her, and she started pulling herself up to her feet, "Mom, what are you doing?" I dropped my backpack and quickly walked to catch her if she were to fall.

"Don't worry, I'm okay, I just wanted to show you that I am moving my legs more," she said, standing up, but still gripping the table to balance herself. "It's just a matter of time and I'll be back to my old self."

I was so excited; I gave her a hug. Alura also came up and gave my mother a hug.

"How are you, sweet girl?" my mother asked Alura.

"I'm good. It's nice to see that you are able to move your legs again."

"Thank you, they been doing double time with me at physical therapy."

I walked over and pulled two glasses from the cabinet, opened the refrigerator, and pulled out the tea, "Do you want any ice in your tea?" I asked Alura.

"Yes, you can't have iced tea without ice."

"So true!"

"How was school?" my mother asked to no one in particular.

"It was great mom, much better than I had expected!"

"Yeah, it was really good. Ralphie and I have four classes together."

A knock on the front door caught our attention. I went into the living room and opened the door, it was Jaray, "Hey Ralphie, I just wanted to stop by and see if you wanted to go for a ride?" he said, revealing his new car, a brand-new Ford Mustang Cobra, orange with black stripes and black rims.

"What!" I said, on my way outside to look at the car.

"Yeah, I just got it off the showroom floor in Dallas."

"I do want to go for a ride!"

"Let's go!"

"Let me get Alura," I turned to find Alura and my mother on the porch already looking at the car.

"Jaray, you got me a new car?" my mother asked, sarcastically.

"In your dreams, Aunty Barb!"

"Alura, do you wanna go for a ride?"

"Sure. Barb you want to come, too?" Alura asked my mother.

"I do."

We all got into the car, me and Alura in the backseat which didn't have much room, my mother in the passenger seat, and Jaray behind the wheel. We left my mother's wheelchair in the driveway and went cruising around town. Jaray played Tupac on the stereo and he had heads turning right and left looking at us. I saw Officer Madison even do a double-take and thought he would come to pull us over, but he just waved and kept going. We cruised downtown and hit some back roads, it was nice, mom enjoyed it, too. Alura and I sat in the back seat holding hands the whole time.

Jaray took us back to my house and dropped us off. Alura and I walked to her house, she kissed my cheek and went inside. I was shocked, but I wanted more. I left there and walked by Daron's but didn't stop. The sky was starting to get dark and I could see the living room light on in Jarod's house. His granny sitting in a reclining chair, I didn't hear any music this time. The green screen door still speaking to me. When I reached unc's road, I stopped for a moment, if only just to think. I could turn and go home, or I could head over to unc's and hang with Jaray a bit. Or, I thought, I could just walk for a while and clear my head. Then I thought against it and I chose to walk home and write. The typewriter only made it to my room and my story needs to be told. People need to know that sometimes, things are not always how they seem. People want to fool those around them in order to keep their power.

We've moved to Grayson for a better future, my mother told me. She had secured a better paying job, so we could afford the better things in life. We were starting that better life before someone wanted to take it away from us. Someone who wanted more power and control. Someone who judged me by my skin color and not by who I was. They didn't care if they killed the wrong black person. If they'd cared, they would have done more research and found that I wasn't the kid they thought I was and probably would have killed Jaray making it look like it was done by members of the KKK. They wanted to fool others into thinking the death was about racism, which in a way, it was about racism, only, they hadn't succeeded.

I have to thank them, though, because they've taught me a valuable lesson, that is: Nothing is ever what it seems. People are evil, but we all know that people can change, and people can change their surroundings. All we have to do is stand together, black, white, brown, red, all colors, together we can change the world. If we stand in groups of one color, where does that put those like me who are biracial? Alone? We should stand together, strong, all colors together against racism, against business empires that want to control everything. With God, we have the power to do anything. The power to keep our freedom. We can do away with the River Roads, gangs, corrupt organizations, and politicians.

I sat in my room all night writing, pecking away on the typewriter Daron had loaned me. I may not have been in a consistent battle of racism but being hung at fourteen sure tops the list. I was lucky, not many people were or are as lucky as I was. I've heard stories of people being killed over their skin color, their heads being cut off and hung on poles. How can people be so evil and pretend that it was okay to do something like that?

"Ralphie, could you come and help me for a minute?" my mother asked me through my bedroom door.

"Sure mom."

I walked out and she was turned around toward the living room, "I have this book that has house blueprints and I want you to help me find one that we can have built. Jaray is going to build us a house and I'll pay him back out of my paycheck."

"Okay, that sounds great. When did you get this book?"

"Jaray just dropped it off and said I could have any house I wanted, and he would hire someone to build it on one of his properties."

"I love Jaray, he has such a big heart even though he acts so tough."

"Yes, he does."

We've spent the rest of the night going through the blueprints and decided on the one with four bedrooms and two bathrooms, wheelchair accessible and we also decided to have a pool, and a pool house, so I could swim anytime I wanted to.

"I'm going to go to bed now," I said, giving my mother a hug.

"Okay, Ralphie, I think I'll go to bed, too."

I went into my room and sat down in front of the typewriter. I've only written twenty pages and figured I could write some more before actually going to sleep. I wanted to get this out of my head and on paper. The typewriter sure did speed up the process.

I woke up a few hours later and found myself still sitting in front of the typewriter. I got up and went into the kitchen to get me something to drink. The refrigerator light shining throughout the kitchen and dining room. I poured myself a glass of tea and drank most of it before putting the glass in the sink.

"Ralphie, are you okay?" my mother asked, startling me.

"Yeah, I was just thirsty."

"I heard something outside and got up to see what it was then heard you in here."

"You heard something outside?"

"Yeah," she said, wheeling her chair to the window and looked out. "I don't see anything, though."

"Maybe it's the wind," I said and then someone had bumped the side of the house.

My breath froze and my heart jumped. There was someone outside of our house. My mother picked up the phone from the wall and dialed the police.

"Grayson Police Department," I heard them say.

"This is Barbara Morre, there is someone outside our home, they just hit the side of our house," she said quickly in the receiver.

"Okay Mrs. Morre, we're sending an officer, does anyone need any medical attention?"

"Not at the moment."

I found myself looking out the windows to see if I could see anyone, but there was no one to be seen. We heard the thump against the house again but in a different area. The lights in the house were still off so they couldn't see us. My mother still held the phone in her hand, "I just heard them hit the side of our house again," she said to the dispatcher.

"I think I heard it, too," the dispatcher said.

This time I wished I had a gun; I didn't know who was out there and what they were trying to do. I felt if I had a gun I could go out and fire a few warning shots and that would scare them off. Before I finished my thought, I saw a police car pull up and an officer jump out, another police car pulled up and another officer jumped out. They had both gone in different directions around my house. I heard them yell *freeze*. A moment later I saw them come around to the front of the house with a man handcuffed. They placed him in one of the police cars and then one officer came to the door. We opened to find him out of breath.

"Mrs. Morre, we apprehended someone in your backyard. He was drunk. It appeared he was trying to relieve himself. He says he lives here," the officer said.

"No, he does not live here," my mother said.

"Okay, ma'am."

The police officer told us to have a good night and both officers left.

"A drunk man in our backyard trying to relieve himself," I said, shaking my head.

"Doesn't make any sense to me," my mother said.

Knock, Knock!

"Who's that knocking?" my mother asked.

I peeked out the window and saw a small lady standing on the porch. I opened the door, and I could see she was crying and looked a little beat up.

"Could I help you?" I asked.

"Yes, my husband is drunk, and he has beat me up and I don't know where he is, but I want to know if I could use your phone to call the police, he ripped mine out of the wall."

"Yeah, come in," I say stepping out of the way to allow her to come inside. My mother came over to her, "The phone is on the wall, but I think the police have arrested your husband already, I think he was in our backyard."

"I'm sorry," the lady said.

"No, it's not your fault."

The lady picked up the phone and dialed the police. I could hear the dispatcher pick up and the lady told them what had happened, and they said they'll send a car. She hung up the phone.

"Could I sit?" she asked, pointing to the couch.

"Absolutely. Do you want something to drink?" my mother asked.

"Yes, some water if that's okay."

"That's fine, Ralphie, get her some water, please."

I walk into the kitchen, pull out a clean glass and fill it with water for the lady. My mother was still talking to her, the lady had told my mother her name, Terry.

"Terry, the officer will be here at any moment," my mother said, and I heard a door shut. I got up and went to the door, the officer was almost to the front door when I opened it up.

"We've got a call about a domestic," he said.

"Yes, she's in here," I said, stepping out of his way. He walks in and pauses, "Ma'am, you called us?"

"Yes, my husband got drunk and started beating on me," Terry said, crying.

"Okay, ma'am," the officer said, pulling out a pad to write on.

"Who is your husband?"

"Allan Roberts," she said.

"I know Allan," my mother told them. "I went to school with him."

Terry answered all the questions the officer asked, and he offered to give her a ride home or to someplace. She declined and said she only lived next door.

"Terry, you can stay here if you want, sleep on the couch. You are not going to put me or Ralphie out."

"Thanks, but I think as long as Allan is in jail, I will be okay at home."

"Okay, then."

I went back to my room and left them two in the living room. I don't understand how someone can beat up on someone they love. That just doesn't make any sense to me. Some people are just out of their mind which makes way for the devil. I've heard my grandma say one time that the devil is roaming around the world seeking souls he can devour. When someone is drunk, they lose control of their mind and the ol' devil makes his way in and makes them do stupid things like, beat up someone they supposedly love. It's pitiful. There is some good that came out of this whole deal, though, my mother gained a new friend. She needed someone other than family to talk to.

I finally got myself into bed and went to sleep. I slept well through the night and the next morning I got up to mom and Terry drinking coffee together. They were laughing and joking and cracking each other up.

"Good morning, Ralphie, how did you sleep?" my mother asked.

"Good morning, I slept great, actually. The best I've slept since we've moved here."

"That's great, I'm glad to hear that, I slept great, too. Grab yourself some breakfast, Terry cooked it this morning."

"Okay." I looked into the kitchen and noticed scrambled eggs, bacon and jelly toast. I poured myself some coffee and made myself a plate and sat down at the kitchen table, when I heard someone knock on the door. Terry went over and opened the door.

"Hello, I'm Kelly James, from the Grayson Sun."

"It's Kelly James from Grayson Sun," Terry said looking over at my mother.

"Okay, let her come on in."

"Hello Ms. James, I'm Barbara Morre, how can I help you?"

"Ms. Morre, I've heard…"

"Call me Barbara, please. Have a seat," my mother said pointing to an empty spot at the kitchen table.

"Thanks Barbara," Kelly said, walking in the house.

"Have a seat, would you like something to drink?"

"No, nothing to drink for me, thank you so much. I just wanted to ask you a few questions about what happened to you and your son, if that would be all right."

"Yes, that's fine. How did you know about that?"

"Well, the police have to report their arrest and traffic stops for the public and I'd noticed a pattern. Then the transfer of ownership to Jaray Morre, I called him up and asked him some questions, which led me to you and your son."

My mother, shaking her head, said, "Jaray. I should have known."

"Yes, he wouldn't tell me much, he says that Ralphie is writing about it."

"Yeah, Ralphie likes to write and has been writing his story using a typewriter he borrowed from a friend. Ralphie, let's give Ms. James a story to tell the people okay."

"Okay," I said, taking a bite from my last piece of bacon, licking the bacon grease off my fingers. I placed my plate in the sink and washed my hands. I walked back into the dining room drying my hands on the hand towel mom keeps hanging in front of the sink.

"Hi, Ralphie, I'm Kelly James, from the Grayson Sun," she said, with a slight wave.

"Hey," I said, thinking about her name Kelly James and wondered if she had any relation to Jesse James and then leaned against the table where my mother was sitting. Then I sat back down at the table.

"I just wanted to share your story with the people," she said. "When I had found out about it, I just knew I needed the story. There have been many hate related crimes here since the birth of the city back in the early 1900s."

"My friends have told me some stories. Mine wasn't exactly about racism, though. It was some members of the Evanson's Salt Company board that wanted me dead because they thought I was Jaray."

"I've heard. Jaray told me something like that."

"Will this story be limited just to the Grayson paper?"

"Yeah, but I think I'll call a reporter in Dallas after I publish it, and he'll probably cover it, too."

"Good, because the world needs to know," I said, frankly.

"Your mom says that you are writing about it."

"Yeah, I started writing from the beginning, you know, since after moving here."

"Could I read what you have written and pull some of my story from it?"

"Sure. I'll go get it, could you make a copy and give mine back?"

"I sure could."

I went into my room and gathered all the papers, even my notebook I first started writing in and brought them into the dining room.

"Here, it's not organized right now, sorry about that."

"No, that's fine, I will put it together as I read it."

Kelly James stuck around for about two hours. She did eventually get that drink my mother offered her when she had first come in. Terry sat quietly during the whole talk; I mean quietly, never said anything except for the occasionally agreeing. I found out that Kelly is related to Jesse James, she said he is her great great uncle. Her original maiden name is actually Parker, but she had it changed to James when she turned eighteen. She thought that would make her more appealing as a reporter and she could tell people about her heritage. She said some people like to say that they met a member of the Jesse James family and had them in their home. I guess I'm sharing that with you now. I had a relative of Jesse James in my home. It's not as cool as it sounds though, she didn't even know her great great Uncle Jesse James.

# CHAPTER 17

# IN CONCLUSION

K elly James's story came out in the paper a couple of weeks later. She titled it, "A Corporate Lynching," which I thought was a little lame. It made sense, though. Many people were talking about it around town. She did contact her friend in the Dallas news area and he also ran the story, but it was buried in the middle of the paper. I don't know if anyone has actually read it. I'm glad I'm writing my own story because I think people need to hear that some people in power do evil things to keep their power and blame it on society's worse problems. It only makes things worse for everyone including themselves. They may not see it at first, but in the end, it screws us all. They just sit in their big fancy offices and count their dollars they make because of all the chaos. Maybe I read too much into things. It's totally possible. However, things have been great, lately.

Everyone around my family has been a big help, including Terry she has helped with my mother since they've first met. They're like two peas in a pod and have been spending every day together. She has helped my mother with her walking, by getting up every morning and going for a walk. My mother hardly ever uses the wheelchair anymore. Which I think is great. She's always been independent, and it must have been hard for her to have to depend on people so much.

Jaray has set up his board of directors for his new company and its mainly family except for Dexter, his lawyer. Jaray's new company has hired a fencing company to start fencing off Crain's Ferry starting just before my house -- well my old house, we've got a bigger one now, I'll talk about it later. There is a nice big gate going up across River Road as I write this and there is a sign that says, 'Keep Out! This end of River Road is under new ownership and is no longer open to the public.'

Jaray keeps busy with his company, he continues to be homeschooled, but I don't think it'll be for long. He keeps talking about getting a GED. He calls it a *good enough diploma,* which I thought was very funny. He has gained a nickname as well, Scarface, because of the scar where he had the seventeen stitches. Everyone wants him to get it fixed but he refuses, he likes the name Scarface. Many times, he'll say, "Say hello to my little friend!" in the best Al Pacino voice he can while pointing to the scar on his face. He is such a character. My cousin, my brother.

Now, about our new big house. We almost have everything moved over there. I stayed a few nights there with Daron and Jarod in the new house. It's twice the size of the house on River Road and best of all, it's not on River Road, it's on Summertime Street. We have a circle drive, and my mother has a new car that she paid for with the money from her new secretary job at JaMorre Properties, Inc. She wouldn't accept anything more; a secretary is what she's done for a living for over twenty years. Jaray loves it, too, she takes care of him and does more than a regular secretary would. We have a giant pool, but it hasn't been completed yet. After it's finished, it'll be great. I'm going to have a party first thing!

"Ralphie, are you coming?" my mother asked me while walking into the living room.

"Yeah, I just want to finish up here, really quick," I say still typing away on Daron's typewriter.

"Okay, but I want to get going and catch the construction crew before they leave. I want to give them these cookies I've baked."

I shake my head, "Mothers and their cookie baking."

The school here has been better than I had thought it would be, the guys I thought would be trouble are actually surprisingly good kids. We hang out from time to time, they play football, and after the games we all go and hangout often on the weekends, but never at Crain's Ferry. That's where the kids used to go and get drunk and whatnot. Not anymore, though. The school has more people of color now, after the newspaper ran my story, black people from all over moved here and it has really started to change the culture, for the better in my opinion. I've seen some people acting like gang members with tattoos, wearing baggy pants. They are mainly white boys, and they would have these chrome teeth in their mouth they're calling grills. They got them from some rapper guy in Dallas. I thought it was crazy, but it's a thing, I guess. Jaray even got him a pair, too. He looks ridiculous.

Alura and I have been getting remarkably close and spending a lot of time together. I think I may ask her to marry me, when we get older of course. I'll be fifteen soon, yes, I know that's not old enough. My mother says that I should be able to get a permit to drive in about another six months. I can't wait to be able to drive, then Alura and I can cruise around by ourselves, without Jaray or my mom. He has been coming over and we, Alura and I ride around with him all the time in his car. Alura is not as tough as Jarod had said she was, at least not around me. She has never done anything to me that would make me think she is anything but a sweet, beautiful girl. Always jumping in my lap over a bug or something, asking me to kill it and save her. The bug could be smaller than a speck of dust and she'll scream for me to kill it. I always laugh at her, but sometimes, I think she really is scared of those things. Daron says it because she wants a reason to be closer to me, he's probably right. I don't mind, though. I'll kill as many bugs as she wants me to as long as I can be with her.

Daron is becoming more of an activist than a preacher like his father. He says that he feels his calling is to bring attention to the racism in the world. He uses my story a lot. I myself want to just stop talking about it, but then, I'm writing my story about what happened here on River Road. He talked about races being divided. When a race is separated, where does that put us with one white parent and one black parent? We should stand together not as different races but as one race, the human race. I can say I'm white, but because of my skin color, everyone still would call me black. How should I deal with that? I mean, look at Jaray, he can say he is black all day long, but because of his skin color, everyone would just call him a white boy. It bothers him, too. I don't know if it would ever change, but all we can do is spread awareness. I'm black, I'm white, I'm human.

Jarod is preaching a lot more. He has come over countless times to use the typewriter to write his sermons. He is always talking about God and inviting everyone to church next Sunday. That's exactly how he says it, too. "You should come to church next Sunday!" He incorporates racism and such things like that in his sermons. He is turning out to be a really great preacher. He says he may even take over as youth pastor soon if Pastor Mike asks him to. We've actually become very good friends, probably even closer than Daron, and I. Don't tell Daron I said that. Although, I think he knows that by now. Jarod and I spend a lot of time talking about everything under the sun and moon. He's an avid reader as I am, we spend countless hours in the library searching for the best books and playing on the computers. A free education, minus the late fees.

Speaking of an avid reader, Mac, my principal back in Harken, he called me a few months back. He said he had heard about what happened from the Dallas paper. As I said, he's an avid reader. Anyway, he told me about him dealing with racism growing up and that his family, his grandparents, were actual slaves. They lived on plantations and everything, working in the fields all day every day. The only way they were able to escape was because of American law changes. That's the way we fight in America, we read up on the laws and have our politicians change them or make new laws and pass them through Congress. Shoot, we could even run for Congress ourselves and change things for the better of all Americans, including black Americans. I was called an African American once and I was disturbed by that because I'm not from Africa. I may have some family from there, but I'm American, born and raised here in America. I should be called a Native

American. Those are some things that need changing I guess, or maybe not. But I feel that if people keep calling us black people who are born in America, African Americans, then what do they call people from Africa who move here and become American citizens? African Americans right, skin color doesn't matter, or does it? There are white Africans who came to America and now are American citizens. Are they called African Americans? If I have never even been to Africa, why should I be called an African? I should just be called an American.

All I can do is tell my story. I don't want to just sit idle and do nothing about how our people are being treated. My people are both black and white. I favor my father more than I do my mother and that's okay with me. My father may not have been in my life, but that doesn't mean that I don't care for him. I can only imagine the struggles he has gone through in his life, being a black man in America. He may not have been there for me and sometimes I believe it partially isn't his fault. The American struggle for a black man is surviving in a white man's world. The American dream is as Martin Luther King said in his, *I have a dream*, speech.

"Today, I have a dream, and the dream is for not only white and blacks to hold hands, but for all people to come together as one people."

# CHAPTER 18

# JARAY'S AFTERWORD

After Ralphie moved to Grayson, we've spent a lot of time together. His story doesn't reflect all of it but a short time right after he moved here. Once when he and Aunty Barb came to visit, Ralphie even went and got himself a library card. He loves to read, and he would always bring something to read while they were here during their visits. He would check out books from the library and read after everyone went to bed. Aunty Barb was already talking about moving here because she was hired by Evanson's Salt Company, after being interviewed twice. Those board members, after Farren stealing and copying Mr. Evanson's will, thought that Ralphie and Aunty Barb were who the will was talking about. I was the negro descendant who lived with the white woman, Aunty Janie. I don't know why they just didn't say white family, the will didn't mention anything about unc, just a white woman. Maybe to throw people off. Mr. Evanson was smart in doing what he did. He knew that someone would try and do something and figured he'd hide my true identity from everyone. Doing so caused confusion with them thinking Ralphie was me because I never looked like I was mixed. My skin tone is white, and no one has ever thought I was anything but that. Ralphie has a little more color and couldn't pass for being white. Nor would he want to, even after what happened to him.

When Ralphie told me about him writing his story about what had happened to him because of some greedy corporate crackers, I thought he was nuts. Why would he want to be writing about such a terrible time in his life? After reading a copy of the story he had brought me, I've realized that his story is really about him trying to understand why people judge by a person's skin color and he's determined to find a way to change that. At first, I'd thought he may have a misunderstanding that gangs and the Klan were the same, they are not. What he was saying, though, was that they both judge by color. When you judge by the color of someone's skin, you miss the perfect opportunity to get to know someone. To get to know another human being. Hate isn't something someone inherits, it's something that is taught. Ralphie and I were never taught to hate anyone and when he was discriminated against, whether it was by gangs for what he was wearing or by white people for the color of his skin, he didn't understand why people hated color so much. After finding out the attack on him wasn't entirely about racism, he still felt that people needed to hear his story. They'd lynched him and he survived to talk about it. Many black people were lynched in the past, and no one even knew about it. I'd bet my fortune that many still are today, yet it isn't brought up. Keeping black people down and treating us as if we were nothing more by the lower race. I've heard people say just stop talking about racism in America and it will go away. To do away with Black History Month. But what they don't understand is that not talking about the issue would only keep a lid on what they are still doing to us today. Maybe in the future it will get better for us. Perhaps even elect a black president. Tupac said we are not ready to see a black president. I would have to say otherwise. Having a black president might help America grow together. We all need to spread love, not hate. I must sound like a hippie, but as King says, "Love is the only force capable of transforming an enemy into a friend." Whether they are a member of another gang or another race or another religion, they are people looking to be loved. People will do anything for love or to be loved by someone. I wouldn't miss an opportunity to be close to my mother when she was around, even if she was only around for money to buy more booze. And while she was there, I was looking for her love. Since she wasn't taking care of me, I was practically raised on music, by my favorite rappers, because my mother did not take the time to get to know me, to love me. She thought about the racist rapist when she saw me. I hated that, and she said she didn't but, I know better. Seeing me was a reminder of a trauma she'd experienced, and it may take a lifetime to heal. Racism runs deep and touches people for generations. Not talking about it probably would help but not talking about it could also make racism worse. Ralphie and I haven't seen too much racism and this book may shine a light on that fact. Our family is not racist and has been called that by other black folks just because of where we live. Ralphie said that a city is made up of its people, which is true. Grayson today is still predominantly white and there is still racism here. But there are people here that are not racist and are still treated as such, not because of the color of their skin but because they live here in Grayson. I'm one of those people.

After I inherited the estate from Mr. Evanson, I made some major changes. The first thing on my list was to do something about River Road. There has been too much activity down at Crain's Ferry over the many years Grayson has been a city. The Klan used to host rallies there and they've lynched many black and white people by the river. I'd put money on it, that there are many bodies in the Saline river. Ralphie was luckily not one of those bodies. So now, when people want to go down to Crain's Ferry, they can't. That place is fenced and gated off to the public. I don't want anyone down there and we don't even go down there anymore. I have people that work for me taking care of the property and running cattle. I couldn't do it even if I wanted to. I'm no cowboy. Plus, I have better things to do than to spend my life running cattle. I have a family to take care of, both black and white.

My mother took the time to get to know me better and we work together now at JaMorre Companies Inc., she is my

Chairman of the Board. People thought she only did it for the money, but what they don't know is that she works for a paycheck like everyone else. I didn't give her any special treatment aside from providing her with help for her addiction. Which, I do offer to all other employees at JaMorre Properties.

I hope that you get something out of this story Ralphie wrote. He has been through some tough stuff over the last fifteen years. Things that some kids shouldn't have to deal with, such as being lynched and surviving to talk about it. Ralphie is strong and God has a plan for him. Maybe to become the first black president of the United States, move over Bill Clinton. Maybe his calling is to bring light to the River Roads around the world. This is his story, his story on River Road.

# ACKNOWLEDGMENTS

First and foremost, I want to thank God. Without God, I would not be writing, or breathing for that matter. Thank you. I want to thank my daughter, Keish for her wonderful conversations about the characters in River Road, her input is unquestionable. My wife, Marie, for her criticism, without it, I'd still be writing River Road. Thank you, Angelica, for your editing, you make my work so much better. I want to thank everyone else that had to listen to me talk about my book, even though their faces made me think they did not care to hear it. Thank you for listening anyway, it helped me with the development of the story for the book.

www.ingramcontent.com/pod-product-compliance
Lightning Source LLC
Chambersburg PA
CBHW031718170626
46808CB00005B/1800